THOMAS GREANIAS

RED GLARE

D1730789

Atlantis Ink
NAPLES, FLORIDA

ATLANTIS Ink

Atlantis Ink
780 Fifth Avenue South
Naples, Florida 34102

Publisher's Note: This is a work of fiction. Names, characters, places, and incidents are a product of the author's imagination. Locales and public names are sometimes used for atmospheric purposes. Any resemblance to actual people, living or dead, or to businesses, companies, events, institutions, or locales is completely coincidental.

Cover Design by Ana Grigoriu-Voicu
Book Layout by Book Design

Red Glare / Thomas Greanias -- 1st ed.
ISBN 978-1-7350856-1-6

For such a time as now.

CHAPTER ONE

0500 Hours
Offutt Air Force Base
Omaha, Nebraska

Every minute of every day since February 3, 1961, a Strategic Command "Looking Glass" plane carrying an Air Force general has been circling the Midwest, ready to seize control of America's nuclear arsenal should a surprise attack destroy command posts on the ground. The program officially ended with the Cold War, but actually carries on under various guises and aircraft. Only once, in the skies of September 11, 2001, has a Looking Glass plane ever been spotted by the general public. Even then the Pentagon denied its existence.

This morning it was General Brad Marshall's turn to play God.

Marshall gazed at the converted military Boeing 747-200 "Doomsday" jumbo jet waiting for him in the pre-dawn darkness as his black Chevy Suburban, wipers working furiously, braked to a halt and he stepped out.

The ice on the tarmac crunched under his brisk, powerful strides. The snow was coming down harder now. He turned up the collar of his overcoat and bore through the curtain of white to Looking Glass, its gigantic GE 80-series engines winding up to takeoff power. Originally, the plane was an EC-135C, then an E-6 Mercury. The new model, a modified E4-B conscripted from Operation Nightwatch, had triple the floor space and was practically a dead ringer for the president's Air Force One. Only the small white dome on top betrayed its enhanced military capabilities.

So, this is what Siberia feels like, Marshall thought, both of the bitter cold and his new obscure-if-critical posting. A "promotion to general" hatched by an insecure president to keep a war hero as far away as possible from TV crews.

At the base of the tall stairs leading up to the six-story-high plane stood an intelligence officer Marshall had never seen before in person. Marshall recognized him from a video briefing somewhere, despite the ridiculous N95 face mask he was wearing.

The officer saluted as he approached. "General Marshall, sir."

Marshall frowned. "What happened to Colonel Reynolds?"

"Virus, sir." The intelligence officer pointed a thermometer at his forehead. "I'm Colonel Quinn. I'll be your second."

Marshall looked Quinn over. He had handpicked the Looking Glass crew himself, and this ringer was second-string at best. The switch wasn't entirely unexpected, but Marshall was annoyed that General Carver at STRATCOM hadn't bothered to give him an official heads-up about such a critical assignment. It only confirmed just how routine and insignificant these flights had become to the Department of Defense.

"Any other changes, Quinn?" Marshall said as he started up the steps. "Are all the surfaces sanitized? Are the HEPA air filters recycling properly? Are all the airmen in Hazmat flightsuits? We wouldn't want anybody catching a cold or sniffle."

"Oh, yes, sir," Quinn said eagerly until he realized Marshall was mocking him. "Just following procedures."

Marshall worked his way through the main deck's various compartments—a command work area, conference room, briefing room, an operations team work area, and a secondary communications compartment. Not a mask in sight. With a confident smile he acknowledged their salutes and heartfelt greetings.

Inside the communications center, Major Brianna Thompson lit up when Marshall entered, Quinn right behind.

"General Marshall, sir," the curvy redhead said.

"Major Tom," Marshall replied. "Threat alert status?"

She handed him a report. "Orange, sir."

Marshall looked it over. "Flight forecast?"

She looked him in the eye. "Clear skies, sir."

Marshall nodded, but Quinn looked confused as he glanced at the dark clouds. "The President, Major. Give me his twenty."

"Back in Washington with everybody else for tonight's State of the Union."

"Not everybody," Marshall said, handing back the report.

She nodded and said softly, "You deserve better, sir."

"Don't we all?" Marshall said and marched off.

A couple of armed Looking Glass officers were already waiting in the battle staff compartment when Marshall entered and sat down in his general's swivel chair.

"Harney, Wilson." Marshall nodded to the men. "Welcome to Air Armageddon. Please present your boarding passes."

The young officers dutifully surrendered the nuclear authenticator codes they were carrying.

Marshall removed the key he wore around his neck and inserted it into one of two locks in the red steel box next to his seat. "Colonel Quinn?"

"Sir." Quinn, still hurrying in behind Marshall, produced his own key and inserted it into the second lock.

Marshall opened the double-padlocked safe.

"As you gentlemen know, a Looking Glass plane like ours is always in the air." Marshall paused to look each officer in the eye. "In the event of surprise nuclear attack, we can command American forces from the air and launch our ICBMs by remote control. Colonel Quinn, as my second officer, you are watching me place the nuclear authenticator codes in here for safekeeping."

Marshall placed the code cards that Harney and Wilson had given him inside the safe, next to the two launch keys that together could unleash the

Apocalypse. He locked the double padlocks with the safe keys. He hung the long chain of his key to the safe around his neck again. He then pocketed Quinn's second key.

"God forbid we'll ever need these."

Marshall turned his attention to a pre-flight checklist. Wilson and Harney stood like statues on either side of him, emotionless. But he could feel Quinn's stare.

Quinn cleared his throat. "Sir."

"Yes," Marshall said without looking up. But he could hear the uncertainty in Quinn's voice.

"The other key, sir."

Marshall played it cool. "What about it, Quinn?"

"Regulations state that both keys are not to be in the possession of a single officer," Quinn said, sounding forced.

Marshall knew that this kind of situation could throw even the most seasoned officer, and Quinn was hardly that. "I know the regulations," Marshall replied evenly. "I think we have too many regulations these days, don't you?"

Just then Major Tom appeared. "General Marshall," she said, "the tower has cleared us for take-off."

Marshall handed her his checklist and locked eyes with Quinn. "Who's our pilot today, Quinn?"

Quinn did his best not to look at his tablet. It took a few seconds, but he got it right. "That would be Captain Delaney, sir. And Rogers is co-pilot."

Marshall nodded. "Trained them myself. Just like the rest of the crew. Everybody but you, Quinn. We don't just look out for each other. We've made a pact. You know the kind of loyalty I'm talking about, Quinn?"

Quinn said nothing. His eyes were wide, his lips pressed tightly.

"I didn't think so." Marshall turned to his crew and smiled. "To your stations, officers."

Wilson and Harney did as they were told. As did Major Tom.

Marshall heard Quinn unlock his sidearm holster, and when he looked up, he saw the barrel of Quinn's M18 handgun pointed at him.

Quinn said, "Sir, I'm going to have to ask you for that key."

Marshall smiled. His voice turned softer. "You're new to Looking Glass, aren't you?"

"My first flight, sir. But I've flown several times with Colonel Kozlowski aboard the Nightwatch plane."

"Flying with the chauffeur of the president's military limo isn't the same as flying with me,

Colonel. So, if you don't mind, I'm going to keep your key."

"Regulations, sir," said Quinn as his hand holding the pistol trembled slightly.

"I thought you were a team player, Quinn."

"I am, sir. But I insist you surrender the key, or I'll be forced to shoot you."

"Go ahead, Quinn. Make my day."

Quinn looked bewildered. But he took a firmer grasp of his pistol. "On the count of three, sir. Three…"

Marshall stared a hole through him and said nothing.

"Two…"

Quinn's voice started to shake again. But Marshall had to admit to himself that the kid could stand his ground.

"One…"

Marshall's face broke into a wide grin.

"Congratulations, Colonel." Marshall removed the second key from his pocket and dangled it in front of Quinn. "You passed the test."

Quinn grabbed the key with one hand and with his other holstered the M18 and wiped his forehead. "For a minute there, sir, I thought…"

"Yeah, I know," Marshall said. "You thought I was flipping out. Next time, pull the trigger."

"Yes, sir," Quinn said. "I will, sir."

Marshall tapped his armrest commlink. "Captain Delaney."

The pilot's voice came through on the speaker. "Yes, sir."

"Let's roll."

The engines roared to take-off speed as the Looking Glass plane began to barrel down the runway. A minute later they lifted off the ground and soared into dark skies. *At last*, thought Marshall, the National Airborne Military Command Post was in the clouds where she—and he—belonged.

CHAPTER TWO

0730 Hours
0 Street
Washington, D.C.

The headline in the *Washington Post* read "No Sachs Education for Kids." A photo showed a beleaguered U.S. Secretary of Education Deborah Sachs at a meeting of the nation's governors in Washington. Her deer-in-the-headlights look said it all.

Sachs frowned at the picture of herself. It was above a smaller story about a slain Metro security guard whose body was found in a railyard. She adjusted the AirPod in her ear as she sipped her morning coffee while the TV blared.

"The president is expected to announce the resignation of his outspoken and controversial Secretary of Education after tonight's State of the

Union address," the Today show was saying, and proceeded to recite her most recent run-ins with the Administration. "Moving on to the crisis in the Far East..."

She lowered the volume on the TV to take a call from her friend Lauren at Commerce, who immediately offered her condolences.

"No, he hasn't given me my resignation yet," Sachs said, flicking her freshly cut black hair away to adjust the AirPod in her right ear. She was going to grow her hair out, she decided, now that she no longer required the Beltway cut of a Cabinet secretary. "I have to give it to him this morning. Then he'll accept it tomorrow. Tonight is all about him, remember? All I know is that Nadine has been a super assistant."

Blah, blah, blah. Lauren was such a spin doctor with the excuses.

"Well, could you see what you could do for her just the same? Thanks."

Sachs hung up and stared out the windows at the falling snow. Her Georgetown rowhouse until now had been her sole refuge from the nonsense of Washington. The hunter green walls, white trim and oils over the fireplace had offered an illusion of security and tradition in her otherwise uncertain life.

But it couldn't shield her from urban Democrats who made a federal case for public education while their own children attended private schools, which were the first to fully reopen from the global COVID-19 pandemic. Or from suburban Republicans, whose children could attend quality public schools or simply study online at home, who demanded vouchers for private schools. Or from the nagging reality she had no home to go back to again because Richard was gone forever, and without him it just wouldn't be home. But in the process she was depriving Jennifer.

She was mulling over this last painful thought when her assistant Nadine emerged from the front hallway, immaculate in her latest fashionable suit beyond her pay grade, ready to tackle lobbyists, teachers' unions and Congress. Her dark hair was slicked back. She smiled broadly, keeping up a good front.

"Good morning, boss."

"For some Americans," Sachs replied.

"Told you being a public servant isn't worth the cost after two years," Nadine said, and then stopped. "What's this?" She was pointing to the packed overnight carry-on by the door.

"I'm grabbing the shuttle to see Jennifer," Sachs said. "You book my ticket like I asked?"

"Uh, no," Nadine said. "You're going to see the president and tell him why you should keep your job."

Nadine walked over to the desk and picked up what looked like a student term paper awash in red corrections. In the upper right corner was a big, fat "B."

"And what's this, Madame Secretary?"

Sachs said, "My speech for Jennifer's school assembly."

"You graded yourself?"

"I'll do better on the next draft," Sachs replied without a trace of embarrassment.

"Next draft?" Nadine looked at her Rolex. Sachs had told her to stop with the bling as they were trying to help inner city schools, but it was no use. "Hey, we canceled that speech. You have a meeting at the White House this morning. Why are we still talking?"

"I rescheduled," Sachs told her. "I'm not going to disappoint Jennifer again. School assemblies actually mean something to kids now. Besides, the president is going to cancel on me anyway. He always does. This time permanently. Just text him my resignation."

Sachs grabbed her carry-on and rolled it behind her down the hallway into the wintry day and the waiting government limousine, leaving Nadine to lock up after her. The driver popped the trunk, dropped her bag inside, and opened the rear door for her to get inside where it was warm.

Nadine finished a call at the curb and then climbed in, incredulous. "Only you, boss."

"Meaning what?" Sachs asked her.

"Meaning here you are losing your job on national TV and all you can do is worry about your assistant's ass and some speech nobody's going to hear."

"Jennifer and her friends are going to hear it," Sachs said. "You have a better suggestion?"

"Lecture circuit," Nadine replied. "You might as well get paid for it."

Sachs laughed. "If nobody listened to me when I was Secretary of Education, why would they listen to me afterward? Besides, the whole silver lining is that my New York-Washington commuting days are over. I can spend more time with Jennifer."

Nadine grimaced. "She's what, ten? Give her a year and she'll want you out of her life for good."

"Thank you, Nadine, that's comforting," Sachs said. "She's thirteen and needs me more than ever. Two years is a long time for a girl to live with her aunt. She hates me. If I'm going to be living in New

York again, I'm going to be living with my daughter."

Nadine said, "We'll work something out. Now let's go see the president. Maybe he's changed his mind."

Sachs was firm. "Look, did you book me on the shuttle to New York or not?"

Nadine flashed the email confirmation on her government-issued phone. "I've got you out of Reagan National in forty minutes."

"Nadine, I don't know what I'm going to do without you."

"You go to New York and we're both gonna find out," Nadine warned her. "Because if you don't make it back tonight for the State of the Union, you're gonna piss off the president."

"That's my job, remember?"

"Was your job," Nadine huffed.

Sachs smiled. "I've got a better one now."

CHAPTER THREE

1000 Hours
Hay-Adams Hotel

USAF Colonel Joseph Kozlowski shifted under the covers of the bed. A heavy cloud of despair weighed him down. He reached for Sherry, but she was gone.

Kozlowski turned onto his back and blinked his eyes open. He held up his watch and squinted. Then he slipped out of bed and plodded toward the curtains and pulled them back. The bleak January light seeped in as he looked across H Street at the White House. The snow was still coming down, burying the Rose Garden and Ellipse. He could barely make out the towering spike of the Washington Monument beyond.

Just then he could hear a hair dryer in the bathroom. He smelled coffee and saw that Sherry had room service bring up breakfast for herself. All that was left was some picked-over fruit and a pile of newspapers screaming about yet another crisis in the Far East.

He fished out a melon cube, poured himself some lukewarm coffee and scanned the headlines. It had been awhile since he'd seen an actual newspaper. Only hotels seemed to have them for guests these days, and only politicos like Sherry bothered to read them. Everything was online these days, virtual, fake. Especially the news. Nobody wanted to go on record reporting that China was like Japan in the 1930s, actively engaging in a secret war against and inside the U.S. for years. The whole world was already on its way to hell and would look nothing like it did now by the end of the century. Hell, America didn't even look like it did a decade ago.

He was halfway through his cup when Sherry emerged from the bathroom with her blow-dried blonde hair draped over her terrycloth robe with the Hay-Adams Hotel logo on it, which she left open just enough to remind him why he never turned her down for these hotel hideaways.

Kozlowski said, "Leaving so soon?"

"Got to finish Vanderhall's reaction to the State of the Union address," she said, sliding open the closet door to reveal her Armani suit next to his uniform.

The same uniform he had been wearing for eight years now, still a colonel.

"So where am I going, Sherry?"

"You're going nowhere, Koz."

Kozlowski watched her dress. "You finally figured that out?"

"The snow, doofus." Sherry helped herself to his Purple Heart medal from his uniform.

"What are you doing?"

"The colors go with my jacket," she said as she pinned it beneath the lapel of her blazer.

"You ever been wounded while serving your country?" Kozlowski asked her. "That's what it means."

"I won't lose it." She put on her gold earrings and spoke to him in the mirror. "It's not like it's actually worth anything. Stolen honor is legal now."

It was no use arguing with Sherry. She was 27 and wouldn't understand, he concluded as he watched her grab her Gucci soft leather briefcase and walk out the door, off to more important things like personal advancement.

Kozlowski walked over to his blue uniform and looked at the spot where the missing medal belonged. Sherry was right. It was just clothing, bland at that, with some cheap ribbons and medals.

Cheap like his bosses. Cheap like the promises they made and the company they kept.

Everything he grew up believing—serving his country in the armed forces, the presidency, even the United States itself—no longer seemed mythic, but diminished after the pandemic. There were no rules anymore. The current occupant of the White House was yet another empty suit, and he wondered if America was even capable of producing a leader worth following into battle anymore.

He unbuckled the holster sitting on the closet shelf and removed his sidearm, a .38 standard-issue automatic pistol. He felt its weight in his hand.

Almost ten years of his life had passed in two overseas wars, he realized. Just like that. What could I have been by now? A general like Brad Marshall? Definitely a father if Mary hadn't left him. They could have had three or four kids by now. He could be skiing or having snowball fights in Colorado instead of sitting here, feeling old, used-up, worthless.

He pointed the gun to his head and put his finger on the trigger.

CHAPTER FOUR

1144 Hours
The White House

President Peter Rhinehart paced beneath George Washington on the wall of the Oval Office. He had fifteen minutes before his final meeting with Deborah Sachs, and he still needed to work on his delivery of his State of the Union address.

"And let us not live in the past," he recited, stressing the word "past" like it was bad. "But look forward to the future."

Meaning his own political future, he thought, when the ivory desk phone rang. The LED display flashed: *Chairman, JCS. Line Secure. Top Secret.* It was General Robert Sherman, chairman of the Joint Chiefs of Staff, calling from the Pentagon.

Annoyed, Rhinehart picked up. "What is it, Bob?"

21

"Mr. President, we have a situation."

Rhinehart's morning intelligence briefing had spelled out a number of situations, so he could only guess.

"The SS-20?"

"Yes, sir."

"I'm about to address the American people, dammit, and our friend General Marshall is breathing down my neck in the polls," the president huffed. "I don't have time for any false—"

"Mr. President, NEST teams have confirmed there is a stolen Soviet SS-20 nuclear warhead somewhere in Washington. Now the Russians say they have evidence that the Chinese planted it, and that it is set to detonate in five minutes."

"Five minutes?" Rhinehart frowned. "What do the Chinese have to say?"

"The Chinese say that if anybody's planted a nuke in Washington, it's the Russians or Islamic State proxies."

"Goddammit," groaned Rhinehart. "Every major elected official in America has got to be in Washington. How imminent is the threat?"

As if on cue, a military aide burst through the door carrying a black briefcase —the "football" containing nuclear authorization codes. Rhinehart stared at the attaché, speechless.

"I'll brief you after you're secure in the bunker," Sherman pleaded with him on the phone. "Mr. President, we have no time."

Rhinehart hung up and hurried out of the Oval Office. He brushed past the White House military operator at the switchboard, the football and military aide close behind.

"The vice president just arrived," the operator reported.

"Tell her she's leaving," Rhinehart replied. "Get my chopper to airlift her to Andrews."

"Yes, Mr. President."

"Call Jack and Stan and have them meet me downstairs," the president continued. "Alert conference."

"Situation Room?"

"No. The bunker."

The military operator hit a button on his communications console, sounding an alarm.

CHAPTER FIVE

1145 Hours

The Westchester School
Bedford, New York

The Westchester School in Bedford, New York, was a public charter school, one of America's finest. Sachs sent Jennifer here because she didn't want to compromise herself as a champion of public education by enrolling her daughter in a private school. But at the time she couldn't find an acceptable public school in Washington. Aunt Dina and the Westchester Middle School seemed to be the answer, even if Jennifer called all public schools, local or charter, "government schools." Only now, Sachs wondered if she had sacrificed her relationship with her daughter on the altar of her idealism.

The verdict was waiting for her inside. A sullen Jennifer, arms folded across her chest, sat in the office of Principal Mel Boyle. The school clock said 11:44, a few minutes faster than her own watch, so Sachs was running nine minutes late. Eight minutes of hell from the look on Jennifer's face.

"So why aren't you in Washington, putting other children first?" Jennifer asked without looking up.

"Shhh," Sachs replied with a smile. "Mom's playing hooky."

Principal Melanie Boyle, a Barbie blonde in slacks and heels, walked in. "Nice to see you again, Madame Secretary."

"Principal Boyle," Sachs said.

"Doctor Boyle," the principal corrected her. "Everybody's gathering in the gymnasium. We so appreciate your visit, although I wish it were under better circumstances."

Sachs didn't know if Boyle meant her impending job execution or if she was referring to Jennifer. "Is there a problem?"

Boyle slid a file across her desk. Sachs could see the big fat "F" circled in red. "This is Jennifer's U.S. Constitution final," Boyle explained. "Not only could she not name all of the current members of the president's Cabinet, she couldn't even name one. Not even the Secretary of Education."

Boyle raised a perfectly waxed eyebrow.

Sachs studied the exam for a minute and then put it down.

"Well, I'd probably miss that one, too, if the answer wasn't me," she said. "But you know all the rest, Jennifer. What's going on?"

"Globalization," Jennifer said in all seriousness. "The U.S. Constitution is obsolete. To paraphrase Socrates, I'm not a New Yorker or an American, but a citizen of the world."

If Principal Boyle wasn't just as serious as Jennifer, Sachs would have burst out laughing. But she kept a straight face and addressed her daughter.

"You might think so, darling, until you try to enter another country without a passport.

"What about America?" Jennifer shot back. "We've basically had open borders for years."

Sachs caught Doctor Boyle cock her head as if to tell her, "See what I mean?"

"My point is that most of the world's democracies have constitutions based on ours," Sachs told Jennifer. "And unless you want to live in a police state, and condemn the rest of humanity to the same fate, you'd better learn which way is up so you can defend your rights."

"What planet are you from, Mom?" Jennifer made a dramatic, sweeping gesture with her hand, the back of which still bore an admission stamp from some event. "Look around you. Have you seen this government school? This IS a police state. My Bill of Rights didn't keep the government from sucking in your tax dollars, nor Warden Boyle here from opening my private locker and going through my diary or kicking me out of the school dance last Friday."

"School dance?" Sachs repeated, looking at Jennifer and Boyle. "You never told me about a dance. Did you go with—"

"She was wearing thong underwear," Boyle declared, cutting her off. "Highly visible underwear, I might add."

Sachs stared at her 13-year-old daughter, trying to process this ambush of zingers from Boyle. "You were wearing a thong?"

"Well, duh." Jennifer was non-apologetic. "Everybody at the dance could see my thong after Ms. Vice Squad here lifted up my skirt."

Sachs stared at Boyle. "You looked under my daughter's skirt?"

"Whatever," said Jennifer. "Can we get going already?"

"We should move along," Boyle helpfully agreed, clearly looking to delay the inevitable, ugly parent-teacher conference with Sachs. "Everybody's in the gymnasium."

Sachs looked at both of them, not sure whom she was more furious at. "Fine," she said. "Let's not keep them waiting. I'll deal with you later, ladies. Both of you."

CHAPTER SIX

1147 Hours
The White House

President Rhinehart and his military attaché hurried down a long sub-basement corridor beneath the East Wing. At the end of the corridor stood a Marine guarding a steel door. Rhinehart slid a security card through an electronic key slot next to the door. The red light turned off. A green light flashed on. There was a beep and a loud click. The vault opened. Inside the bunker, the White House chief of staff, national security adviser and assorted military aides were arguing around the conference table. They rose in unison when the president entered and looked around.

Rhinehart said, "Where's Bald Eagle?"

"The Central Locator said all eighteen designated presidential successors were due in town for the speech," said Stan Black, his Chief of Staff. "So I sent the Secretary of Defense to a base inspection in California."

As he spoke, the Marine stepped inside and closed the vault door behind him with a definitive thud, sealing them all inside.

"Lucky for him," Rhinehart mumbled.

Jack Natori, his National Security Adviser, said, "We've got the Pentagon on speaker, Mr. President."

Rhinehart said, "What the hell is going on, Bob?"

General Sherman's voice boomed on speaker. "NEST teams picked up trace uranium in the Metro railyards where a security guard was found dead this morning by D.C. police," Sherman said. "It matches the SS-20 core profile. We think the SS-20 or, more likely, its warhead, came into Baltimore on a freighter and then was offloaded to the train to D.C."

"Where is it now?"

"God knows. Probably in some van cruising the streets as we try to get a lock on its location."

Rhinehart took a breath. This was real. "What else are we doing about it, Bob?"

"Everything, including preparing for a detonation," Sherman said. "Army and Air Force choppers at the Pentagon heliport are airlifting 44 selected personnel. The civilians will go to Mount Weather to establish a new government. The military officers are heading to Raven Rock to conduct the war."

"That'll take thirty minutes," Rhinehart said. "I thought we only had five."

Natori checked his watch. "Four minutes now."

Rhinehart said, "The vice president is taking my chopper to Andrews right now."

Natori shook his head. "She'll barely get off the ground before we disappear in a mushroom cloud."

The military attaché then placed the football on the table, dialed the combination and removed a binder — Federal Emergency Plan D.

Rhinehart stared at it for a long, hard moment. He forgot what the D actually stood for, but it always made him think of "Doomsday." He had reached this point in emergency drills only twice before as president. As seriously as he had taken the drills, neither experience had prepared him for what he was feeling now.

The State of the Union is shit, he thought. It wasn't him anymore, nor his administration, nor the coming election, nor even his wife and children. It was about America and her survival—her military, government and economy. Her future was in peril right now, and if this was his last act as president, he would do anything necessary to secure the fate of the free world.

"Guess we should call FEMA and go through the presidential succession bullshit," he finally said. "Which button am I supposed to push?"

A fresh-faced Army colonel showed him on a console. "This one, Mr. President."

CHAPTER SEVEN

1148 Hours
The Westchester School

Sachs could hear the noise of the gymnasium from a distance as she walked with Jennifer down the long, dim hallway. It did feel like a prison, dammit. Jennifer quickened her pace so that Sachs had to catch up with her. Boyle fell a few, safe steps behind.

"You gonna kick Doctor Boyle's ass?"

"Later," Sachs said. "But it's your ass that started all this."

Jennifer seemed even more sullen. "So that's why you came?"

"Of course not," Sachs said. "You think I'd miss a chance to—"

"Give a speech?"

"See my daughter."

Jennifer said nothing. Their footsteps echoed loudly down the empty corridor. Judge Jennifer had found her mother guilty and would condemn her for her sins for the rest of her life.

Sachs tried again. "How's Aunt Dina treating you?"

"She took off for the Bahamas with her French racing boyfriend," Jennifer said. "I'm alone at the house with old Carla her housekeeper."

"What?" Sachs said, feeling like she was arriving just in time to save her daughter.

"Dad was much cooler," Jennifer said. "You sure she's his sister?"

Sachs said, "Well, you won't have to stay with her much longer."

"I heard. You're getting canned. Hope that doesn't mean I have to put up with The Wuss."

The Wuss was Raleigh Westcott, a man Sachs briefly dated after her husband and Jennifer's father Richard died in a plane crash a few years ago. Sachs looked at her daughter. "You know they don't make them like your Daddy."

"Well, I'm not waiting for Superman anymore," Jennifer said. "Why can't you hook up with someone like Brad Marshall?"

Brad Marshall? Sachs thought. Where did that come from?   Sachs knew Marshall, like most

Americans did, from TV. The general's six-foot-four-inch frame, short blond hair, blue eyes and telegenic face generated trust and fan mail. His cool, reassuring voice instilled confidence. He was the legend from Operation Desert Storm, the one-man army who personally destroyed four of Saddam Hussein's palaces in a renegade attempt to assassinate the Iraqi leader. The Napoleon who returned years later to lead the "Surge" in the Iraq War, and then blamed successive, feckless administrations for allowing Iraq to fall to pieces and the Islamic State to rise like a phoenix from the ashes. These days the popular general was calling out America's leaders for selling out to China, which was true. But he also insisted without evidence that Covid-19, which claimed the life of his wife, was not a naturally occurring virus but a weapon originated in a Wuhan lab. A strong but sympathetic figure, Marshall was the only man on earth the President of the United States feared to face in the coming elections.

Sachs said, "You mean the Great American Pretender?"

"Defender, Mom. The Great American Defender."

"If that's what you call lying to Congress about secretly reviving the Star Wars anti-ballistic missile system in space."

"At least someone is concerned about my welfare," Jennifer said.

Sachs said nothing. Brad Marshall was a dangerous man politically because he was so personally charming—and intelligent. The great red Anti-Trump. Sachs wasn't surprised at her daughter's blatant hero worship. But she was disappointed. She hoped Jennifer was only trying to get a rise out of her.

Jennifer removed the tiny USB flashdrive she always wore around her neck. "I just finished a class report on him. Check him out. He's a total stud, and he's going to be the next president. Ms. Cooper my big lib Constitution teacher can't handle it, and that's why she failed me."

Sachs took the flashdrive and sighed. It was shaped like an action figure—"Fembot Fiona"—from Jennifer's favorite hyper-violent videogame, Red Glare. Fembot Fiona's head came off to reveal the USB plug-in. No Baby Yoda figures for her daughter. Jennifer played the game to be cool with the boys online in "group hangouts," because she wasn't allowed to go on in-person dates and kids didn't go out to the movies much anymore, especially since the pandemic.

Sachs said, "What are you, my online dating app?"

"It doesn't take a village to raise a daughter. Just a mom and dad."

"Right," Sachs said and put it around her neck to show Jennifer she valued anything her daughter had done. "Me and Brad Marshall. I can picture it now. The Second American Civil War."

They turned the corner, and the noise of the rowdy assembly grew louder. Jennifer halted outside the gymnasium, packed with students. Really packed. Sachs was shocked at how close together everybody sat. Although safe, it was still a fairly rare, post-pandemic sight to see in person.

Jennifer said, "Just don't embarrass me."

"I'll try my best, sweetie."

Sachs watched Jennifer bravely walk inside first and was about to follow when her phone vibrated with its distinctive "Death March" tone.

Dang, she thought, feeling like Ferris Bueller caught in the act. It was probably the President, ready to blow a purple vein in his red neck as he screamed at her for standing him up.

Sure enough, the voice on the other end seemed to confirm it. "White House. Please hold."

Here it comes, Sachs sighed. All that was missing was a cigarette and blindfold. "Yes?"

The cold, impersonal voice on the other end said, "This is the White House signals operator for the Federal Emergency Management Agency. I have an emergency message for Secretary Sachs."

"Speaking," said Sachs.

The FEMA operator said, "Please authenticate."

"Look," said Sachs, her body temperature heating up, "if the president wants to fire me, he can tell me himself."

"Authenticate."

"Oh, please," she said. "Hold on."

She rummaged through her purse and fished out an authentication card for the correct response.

"I authenticate," said Sachs, reading the card. "Code-name: GREEN DOVE. Password: JENNIFER."

"Where are you?" asked the FEMA operator.

"The Westchester Middle School in Bedford, New York," Sachs replied. As if they didn't know from her phone's GPS signal.

"An alert warning has been declared," the FEMA operator said. "Repeat. An alert warning has been declared. Please acknowledge."

"Sure, I acknowledge," said Sachs, hanging up. She turned off the ringer and walked into the gymnasium.

CHAPTER EIGHT

1148 Hours
National Military Command Center
The Pentagon

Inside the emergency conference room of the National Military Command Center, battle staff officers seated around a huge T-shaped table concentrated on their built-in consoles linking them to American forces worldwide. Six huge color display screens flashed world maps, charts, satellite overheads and troop concentrations.

Chairman Sherman and the rest of the Joint Chiefs stood on a platform perched above the battle staff. On speaker was the President.

"Mr. President," the Chairman said, "we can confirm that the uranium traces found near Union Station came from an old Soviet-era SS-20 nuclear missile, the last of which was allegedly eliminated under the INF Treaty at the Kapustin Yar Missile

Test Complex on May 12, 1991. The Russian president claims the warheads must have been stolen around the same time as those 100 suitcase nukes we've been tracking the past 20 years. The difference is this warhead is more powerful, with a yield of 150 KIT."

"Meaning what?" the president demanded on speaker. "Give me a damage projection so we can prep out-of-area first-responders to mobilize now in case this thing really goes off."

Sherman hated thinking about the unthinkable, especially since he probably wasn't going to be around to assess the accuracy of his estimate. But the president was right about mobilizing out-of-area FEMA help, even if this only shaved a minute off their response time.

"Within the first second of detonation, Mr. President, the shock wave will destroy even our most heavily reinforced steel and concrete buildings within a half-mile radius," Sherman reported from the graphics on screen. "These buildings will include the Pentagon. Nothing inside this ring will be recognizable."

There was a pause on the president's end of the line, and then, "Casualties?"

Sherman said, "The thermal pulse will instantly kill those in the direct line of sight of the blast.

Those indoors will be shielded from the thermal effect but die as buildings collapse. The real issue will be the fireball that erupts, and wind shifts so far as casualties are concerned. Too early to talk hard numbers. But we caught a break with the snow keeping thousands of federal employees at home today. Our best guess is less than 4,000. Not nearly as bad as it might be, but more than 9/11. It's the symbolism that we'll ultimately have to deal with. We're preparing a military response."

"Response to whom?" Rhinehart demanded. "ISIS? The Russians? The Chinese? We don't even know whom we're fighting. If we're fighting."

Sherman said, "Whoever it is gave us no time to negotiate."

"Agreed," said Rhinehart. "So why warn us at all?"

"Good question, sir." Sherman looked up at a clock—one of three-—on a nearby wall. "A five-minute warning means the nuke would go off at 11:49 a.m.," he said, thinking out loud for his staffers. "Why not noon exactly?"

"The blue line, General!" An aide ran up waving a Metro schedule on his phone. "The Metro stops at the Pentagon subway platform at 11:49. The nuke is coming in on the train."

Sherman grabbed the phone and stared at the screen. There it was. 11:49 a.m. The Pentagon. Sherman checked the clock on the wall. 11:48. His stomach sank. God Almighty, it just felt right.

"The bastards are using D.C.'s own transportation system to deliver their destruction—just like the jets on 9/11 and the anthrax mail on Capitol Hill." Sherman started barking new orders. "Tell Metro to stop all trains and get a strike team down there now!"

Sherman turned back to the secure speaker phone to the White House bunker. "Mr. President, we may have made a grave error. The nuke may not have been off-loaded from a Metro train; it may have been on-loaded. We believe that the Pentagon is the primary target, and it will be an underground detonation. That will save us wind shift factoring, but the Metro tunnels will direct the fallout to all nearby stops, including the U.S. Capitol."

He hung up as a quiet sort of pandemonium filled the emergency briefing chamber during the next minute. No shouting. No shoving. Just an urgent, desperate scramble at the consoles. Nobody was heading for the exits.

"General!" His aide tried to pull him away. "You should get to the bunker!"

"If there's a nuke on that train," said Sherman, "those bunker walls will melt like butter."

"What else can we do, sir?"

Sherman held up one finger and picked up the phone. "Get me the National Archives."

CHAPTER NINE

1148 Hours
National Archives

More than 200 high school students visiting from the Presidential Classroom for Young Americans crowded beneath the rotunda around the gold display showcasing the U.S. Constitution. Thanks to the snow and local school closures, they practically had the place to themselves. Their program leader read from the archives literature.

"Every night at closing time the documents are lowered into a fifty-ton vault designed to protect them from fire, shock, heat, water and nuclear explosion," Ms. Chan recited. "The vault was dedicated in 1952 by President Harry Truman, who called it 'as safe from destruction as anything that the wit of modern man can devise.'"

Suddenly, from down the corridor came a shout.

"Away from the glass!"

Sergeant Wanda Randolph, head of the Capitol Police's special recon and tactics or RATS squad, sprinted across the rotunda's marble floor, waving her 50-caliber sniper rifle to evacuate the screaming, fleeing kids.

She tried to radio her man at the Pentagon as she ran, "Omar!"

"We're on it, boss," Omar's voice crackled in her earpiece. "Find a safe place!"

"Just one more thing," she said.

Using whatever speed was left from her days as a track star at Howard University, Randolph ran the race of her life toward the display, almost knocking over Ms. Chan.

"Take cover!" she yelled.

Randolph hurdled three kids crouched in front of the display in one jump. She unlocked a switch and breathlessly watched the display case sink into the floor and drop down a hardened shaft.

CHAPTER TEN

1148 Hours
Joint Base Andrews

Colonel Kozlowski and Captain Linda Li jogged across the tarmac to the awaiting Advanced Airborne Command Post. Unlike the tamer, civilian Air Force One, the militarized E-4B jumbo jet, code-named Nightwatch, was built to soar over mushroom clouds.

"I was worried we were going to have to take off without you, sir," Li said.

"You saved my life, Captain," Kozlowski told his diminutive communications officer. "Again."

Li smiled. "Any time, sir."

Kozlowski had been staring into the barrel of his gun back at the hotel when the call from Li came in. Out of habit he picked up and heard her clear, chipper voice letting him know there had been a roster change. It seemed that General Marshall was logging a shift aboard Looking Glass that morning, and would the colonel mind reporting to base as a Suburban was waiting for him at the hotel entrance. "Unless you have something better to do, sir," she added.

Kozlowski had looked down at his gun again. He suspected that Brad Marshall was not why she really called. She was always looking out for him, even though he knew she didn't approve of his off-duty life. Hell, how did she even know he was at the Hay-Adams? He swore she was psychic. She called it the spiritual gift of discernment. But she had aroused his curiosity. Brad Marshall was never one to languish in obscurity, even for eight hours. So Kozlowski had switched on his gun's safety and told her he'd be right down.

Now he found that he had arrived in the middle of a full-blown Alert One nuclear situation.

"Where's the president?"

"No time, sir," Li said.

Of course not, thought Kozlowski. He himself would never have made it. God bless Captain Li.

The whine of the engines was deafening now as they approached the towering, 231-foot-long plane.

Li shouted, "We have orders to pick up the Secretary of Defense at Edwards AFB."

Kozlowski nodded as they ran up the hydraulic steps into the belly of the fuselage. They made their way through a long communications section manned by six Air Force officers and then entered the battle staff compartment. Fifteen more officers, conducting their pre-flight checks, saluted.

"Let's get the hell out of here!" Kozlowski shouted and strapped himself into a jump seat.

Li plunked down next to him, breathless. The GE 80-series engines wound up into a deep-throated roar, and the jumbo jet started moving down the runway.

Kozlowski leaned back against his seat as the plane left the ground. He never felt more alive in his life.

CHAPTER ELEVEN

1148 Hours
The White House

President President Rhinehart paced the floor in the bunker while his national security adviser gave him the latest.

"Marshall is on Looking Glass, Mr. President."

Rhinehart nodded. Whatever political challenges the general had presented him, he was a genuine military asset. "And my doomsday plane?"

"Nightwatch just took off from Andrews," Jack Natori said.

"Send Nightwatch to California to pick up Bald Eagle at Edwards," said Rhinehart.

At that moment the tumblers in the vault door began to click-clack. Rhinehart and company looked at each other in surprise.

Rhinehart said, "I thought everyone's been accounted for."

"Everybody has been accounted for, Mr. President," said chief of staff Stan Black.

"Then who's that?" Rhinehart demanded.

All eyes turned toward the vault door as it slowly opened to reveal the bald, bullet-headed Secretary of Defense, Ryan O'Donnell.

"What have I missed?" O'Donnell asked in response to the incredulous stares.

Rhinehart gasped, "You're supposed to be in California!"

"My kid's in the hospital with the flu," the Secretary of Defense explained. "I was going to catch a later flight. Central Locator said we're covered."

There was no response, only horrified expressions around the bunker.

O'Donnell stared back blankly. "What?"

CHAPTER TWELVE

1149 Hours
Metro Station
The Pentagon

The Blue Line Metro shot down the tunnel. The few suits and uniforms inside were oblivious to the flashing red light behind the front axle of the chassis as the train screeched along the rails. Their heads were bowed before their mobile screens when the intercom crackled and the conductor's voice announced:

"Next stop, the Pentagon."

The caution lights lining the edge of the platform ahead began to blink. As the commuters started to queue up, a beam of light from the Metro stabbed out of the tunnel.

Six Special Forces troops burst onto the platform and fanned out, parting the sea of commuters into waves of panic and confusion. Their commanding officer, Lt. Matt Omar was once an Azerbaijani national in Baku, trained by the CIA and Oklahoma National Guard to fight terrorists. Later, Wanda Randolph of the U.S. Capitol Police brought him stateside and helped him become an American citizen. She had argued that anyone already putting his life on the line for America deserved it.

"Down there!" shouted Omar.

On the track, attached to the rail's tie-plate, was a small black box on which an even smaller red light was blinking. The security cameras had missed it.

Omar dove for the device even as the Metro shot out of the tunnel and into the station. He desperately tried to disengage the signal box. He looked up helplessly at his partners a second before the Metro, brakes squealing, mowed him down, tripping the signal box and detonating the nuclear warhead bolted to the train.

Suddenly there was a blinding white flash.

CHAPTER THIRTEEN

1149 Hours
Northern Command
Cheyenne Mountain, Colorado

The deer raised her head from the fresh powder of snow and stood deathly still while the pine trees, dripping white, trembled ever so slightly. Then she scrambled away over a slope past the "Danger! Restricted Area" sign and out of view of the security camera.

Hundreds of feet beneath the earth, behind a giant vault-like door of titanium cut out of the mountain, it was snowing inside too, on the monitors of the command center of the U.S. Northern Command.

USAF Maj. Gen. Norman Block, squat and brash, stared at two giant screens where his bosses used to be. "What the hell happened?"

"IONDS sensors detect a nuclear detonation within the U.S., sir," his senior controller reported. "It's Washington."

Block looked at the reconfiguring screens. The left screen displayed TOT MISL 1 — total number of missiles launched. The right screen displayed TTG +00.00.35 — time to go before detonation. It was the plus sign that made Block's blood jump.

"God Almighty," he said.

What happened next went strictly according to plan as America's so-called Post Attack Command Control System swung into action.

Block picked up the gold phone of the Joint Chiefs of Staff Alerting Network (JSCAN) from the console in front of him.

"Put me through to General Carver at STRATCOM."

CHAPTER FOURTEEN

1149 Hours
Strategic Command
Omaha, Nebraska

Inside the underground command center of the Strategic Command, the gold JSCAN telephone started beeping in SC Commander Duane Carver's office. Carver, a lean, low-key man, picked up and heard the news from Block.

"Yes, sir," he replied and stepped out onto his balcony overlooking a floor half the size of a football field where SAC officers manned their consoles deep beneath Offutt Air Force Base near Omaha. Display screens told them which bombers were in the air, which were sitting on runways and how long their engines had been running. "I'm on it."

Carver hung up and picked up the red telephone to the Primary Alerting System. As soon as he did, an alarm warbled, and a rotating red beacon flashed.

On the surface, sirens blared as blue trucks rushed pilots to their awaiting bombers and tankers already lined up for a quick escape.

"Alert crews to your stations," blared the senior controller's voice over the base speakers. "This is not a drill. Repeat. This is not a drill."

On the runways, B-2, B-52 and B-21 Raider bombers and their supporting KC-46 Pegasus tankers began to blast off in Minimum Interval Take Offs (MITOs), one after another with less than twelve seconds between them, collectively armed with enough nuclear warheads to destroy the world's 25 largest cities.

CHAPTER FIFTEEN

1149 Hours
Looking Glass

The Looking Glass plane had reached its 30,000-foot cruising altitude among the thunderclouds when Marshall heard the ominous *click-clack* of an Emergency Action Message or "go code" print out in the battle staff compartment. Wilson ripped it off and walked it over to him.

"Northern Command confirms a first strike on U.S. soil, sir," Wilson said in a trained monotone stripped of all emotion. "The ANMCC says we've lost the Pentagon, White House and most of the nation's elected leadership."

Marshall read the EAM, his mind racing. Without a star in charge and only a junior-grade skeleton staff, the Alternate National Military Command

Center at Raven Rock was about as valuable now as a call center in Bangalore, India. That left General Duane Carver at Strategic Command, General Norm Block at Northern Command, and himself aboard Looking Glass as the essential National Command Authority to run the country.

They would be contacting him any second now, Marshall thought, when Major Tom's voice came on the speaker from the communications compartment.

"Sir, I've got Generals Carver and Block for you in the conference center."

"I want a launch poll, Major Tom," he told her as he rose to his feet. "I want to know what assets got off the ground, what assets are on the ground and which ones are in the ground. And I want it waiting for me when I get there in thirty seconds."

Marshall found the two faces of his last remaining superiors staring from the big screen when he sat down in the conference center: Block, the squat cigar-chomping warrior from the old schools, and Carver, the tall, wiry egghead from the new. Laurel and Hardy in uniform, except Block was white and Carver was black.

"Damage reports, Marshall?"

"Early reports indicate a ground burst," Marshall said, glancing down at the screen beneath the surface of the table. "One hundred fifty KT. Blast radius three miles. Casualties estimated at about four thousand. Looks like snow kept most nonessential federal workers at home."

"So we caught a break," Block said. "That puppy's bark was worse than its bite."

"I suppose that's one way to look at it," Carver said dully. "Marshall, the launch poll."

Marshall glanced down again. The poll had just popped up. It was everything they already knew, but protocol demanded acknowledgment.

"We've lost the Commander-in-Chief at the White House and the Joint Chiefs at the National Military Center at the Pentagon. But we still have command posts at Northern Command, Strategic Command and the ANMCC at Raven Rock," Marshall reported. "We are the National Command Authority now."

Block looked relieved on screen. "So the actual damage to our ability to fight this war is minimal."

"I suppose so, sir," Marshall said. "General Block, you now have operational launch control of U.S. ICBMs in the ground. I'm your back-up here in the Looking Glass air command. General Carver?"

"All my birds are in the air and my sharks are in the water," he said, referring to U.S. bombers and submarines armed with nuclear warheads. "All awaiting orders, soon as we know whom to strike."

"I put my chips on yellow," said Block. "I bet it's General Zhang and the chinks."

Marshall could see the grimace on Carver's face at Block's derogatory remark, especially as U.S. military had more than its fair share of Asian-Americans serving their country. But Carver was too smart to be politically correct in a state of war and kept his cool.

"From this moment on, everything goes strictly according to our plan per our Post Attack Command Control System," Carver ordered. "Hell, Marshall, you wrote it. What's next?"

"The Nightwatch plane from Andrews is circling in the air until the Central Locator selects a designated presidential successor," said Marshall and pressed his speakerphone. "Major Tom, patch us through to Edwards. The NCA needs to speak to the new president, President O'Donnell."

"Negative, sir," the voice on speaker said at the same moment Wilson walked into the conference room with another EAM printout. If Marshall didn't know better, he could have sworn the impenetrable soldier's lower lip was now quivering.

"This just came in, sir."

Marshall scanned the EAM. Twice. Then he looked up at the big screen and broke the news to Block and Carver. "Central Locator says the SecDef swiped his card at the White House just before the blast. He died with the president."

Block looked stunned. "Then who the hell is the designated presidential successor?"

Marshall had trouble forming the words.

"The Secretary of Education," he said. "Deborah Sachs."

"Deborah Sachs?" Carver repeated, the look of dismay on his face rivaling that of Block's. "Are you sure?"

"Central Locator says so," Marshall said. "As of right now, if she's alive, she's our new Commander-in-Chief."

"Deborah Sachs ain't my Commander-in-Chief," Block said. "Who else have you got?"

Marshall frowned and glanced at Carver on the split screen.

"This isn't a football game, Block," Carver said, quickly getting a hold of himself. "We can't simply sub any quarterback we like from our roster."

"The hell we can't," Block shot back. "This is the goddamn Armageddon Bowl, and Team USA needs to field her best quarterback." Block glared out of the screen at Marshall. "Now, son, who else have we got?"

"We have Percy Carson, the Secretary of Homeland Security," Marshall said, playing along with Block as he tried to figure this nightmare out. "He was in Chicago to face election fraud charges from his stint as senator. The president wanted him out of sight for his State of the Union."

"Good enough for me," Block said. "And a hell of a lot more qualified than Sachs."

Marshall said, "Only problem is that presidential succession goes in the order in which the Cabinet offices were created. And Homeland Security was created after Education."

"Then what about the Speaker of the House, somebody, anybody. How do we know for sure they're all dead?"

"Central Locator says so," Marshall said. "Even if it's wrong, FEMA rules state that if a higher-ranking successor has survived, like the Speaker or Vice President, he or she cannot retrieve the office from the sworn successor. Once Sachs is sworn in, she's Commander-in-Chief."

Block said, "Then we have to see to it that she's not sworn in until we've got somebody better to present to America's people and enemies."

"Careful, boys," Carver warned with unmistakable firmness. "The Constitution trumps any post-Apocalypse game scenarios. Report back in two minutes."

Carver disappeared from view, leaving a fuming Block on the screen.

Marshall said, "You have a problem with the plan, sir?"

"You tell me, Marshall. How does Sachs compute into all your scenarios?"

"She doesn't, sir."

"What the hell does that mean, son?" Block demanded. "You see, unlike you, I'm an old fart who has no plans to run for office, or not run for office, whatever the hell dance you and the president had going on. So I can say whatever the hell I goddamn please."

Marshall bristled at the condescension and looked down at his screen. "Profile says she's a school reformer. The teachers unions hate her. But whatever her own opinions, she kept them to herself when they differed from Rhinehart's public policies. For the most part. She certainly spoke her mind to the president in private, which was probably why he asked for her resignation."

"And now she's the president," said Block. "You're saying she might surprise us and prove tougher on the enemy?"

"I'm saying if Sachs is appointed, she's going to play by the book," Marshall said. "And our playbook is pretty clear. Regardless of who's the president, he or she has only a limited set of response options to choose from. In other words, she's not a factor."

"Not a factor?" Block said in disbelief. "Hell, Marshall. The sight of her alone is going to inspire Beijing to unload everything they've got at us. So don't give me this bullshit that she's not a factor. You better goddamn believe she's a factor. Figure out how."

Marshall crumpled the communiqué in his hand. "Yes, sir."

"God help us if she's still alive, Marshall."

CHAPTER SIXTEEN

1155 Hours
The Westchester School

The federal government can't do everything," Sachs said from the podium in the gymnasium. The floor-to-ceiling windows behind her framed the school's wintry track and field. "But it can do something."

The bored eyes of the students and faculty were glazing over. Sachs could see Jennifer slump even lower in her folding chair.

So much for the lecture circuit.

"Please tell me there's more to the United States of America than a libertarian philosophy of no government, no shared values, no community and the notion that the only moral authority for each of us is ourselves."

That seemed to perk them up, ironically, because the students and faculty stirred.

"That's not a country," she continued with more feeling. "That's chaos."

But all eyes were looking over her shoulder. She turned and blinked as two military Black Hawk choppers with side-mounted machine guns landed on the school green and soldiers in field uniforms jumped out.

Suddenly there was a crash from the opposite side of the gym. A dozen men in dark overcoats and sunglasses burst through the doors into the gymnasium.

Some kid yelled, "It's Rambo!" as the men rushed past Jennifer to get to the podium. The look on Jennifer's face said, "You really did it now, Mom."

The leader of the detail halted in front of Sachs. "Secret Service, ma'am. You are Deborah Sachs?"

"And you are?"

"Special Agent Raghav. May I see your authentication card?"

Sachs rummaged through her purse and presented her card to Special Agent Raghav.

He looked back and forth at her like a passport inspector at Dulles International Airport, like she was on the terrorist watch list. Then, showing no emotion, he returned the card and nodded to the others.

The agents closed ranks in a circle around her. "Please come with us."

Sachs didn't budge. "Where?"

"A secure location, ma'am."

"I'm not leaving my daughter." She looked over at Jennifer, who took a few steps back into the crowd, trying to disappear.

Raghav nodded to two agents. "Grab her."

"I'm not going anywhere with you goons!" Jennifer shouted as they approached her. "I'm staying with my friends." She then shoved a prominent middle finger above the heads of the student body and made a break for the opposite exits, the two agents giving her chase.

"Jennifer!" Sachs called out.

But Raghav and the rest tightened their protective ring around her, lifting her an inch off the floor and forcibly carrying her away.

"Smoker Four," Raghav said into his lapel. "Secure exit!"

The freezing air outside on the school green slapped Sachs in the face. A dozen Green Berets wearing distinctive 1st Special Forces headgear and holding M4 carbine assault rifles guarded the Sikorsky S-70 Black Hawks. The rotors were turning impatiently, screaming to lift off. But the commanding officer, a hulking, pock-faced presence in field uniform and jump boots, halted Special Agent Raghav and Sachs' protective detail with a broad, flat hand.

"I'm Colonel Kyle," the officer said. "This chopper is reserved for Green Dove. We'll take it from here."

Raghav flashed his ID. "Wherever she goes, I go."

"I'm not going anywhere without my daughter and until you tell me what's going on," she demanded, trying to veil her fear.

Colonel Kyle looked like he was about to bark an order but seemed to change his mind when he noticed the sea of faces pressed against the gymnasium glass.

"Green Dove and two agents board Black Hawk One," he ordered. "The rest of the suits, inside Black Hawk Two."

Before Sachs could protest, Raghav shoved her hard into the eleven-seat chopper, then climbed in after her with five Green Berets so she couldn't get out. Kyle was the last to board. He signaled the pilot to lift off.

"This is Black Hawk One to base," the pilot spoke into his radio. "Green Dove is airborne. Repeat. Green Dove is airborne. En route to DZ."

As the Black Hawk lifted off, a furious, helpless Sachs could see students and teachers below, noses pressed to the glass wall of the gymnasium, waving good-bye.

"I'm going to have it out with the president when I see him," Sachs said. "If anything happens to my daughter…"

"Don't worry," Colonel Kyle assured her. "We'll get her."

CHAPTER SEVENTEEN

1200 Hours
The Westchester School

Jennifer and a thousand other students exploded out the front doors to the pandemonium in the pick-up lanes. An army of Range Rovers, Mercedes and BMWs jammed the snow-plowed street in front of the entrance. Mothers and a few fathers were screaming for their children.

Jennifer slogged across the slushy parking lot as fast as she could. But now two Green Berets in field uniforms and M4s were gaining on her, and a line of waiting cars stood in her way.

The touch of a hard combat glove on her back prompted her to scream and leap head first across the icy hood of a Mercedes, sliding off into the snow.

She barely had time to look up before she saw a Volvo careening toward her, brakes locked, skidding on the ice. She rolled away seconds before it crashed into the Mercedes.

Getting up, she looked back to see the Marines on the other side of the cars, pointing at her. They split and came at her from both sides, stymied by the panic in the streets.

She turned to run away when a silver minivan braked to a halt in front of her, stopping her cold. Jennifer held her breath as the door slid open automatically and the driver's window rolled down at the same time.

Behind the wheel was her prom date, Robbie, who had given her the red thong for the dance. "Get in!" he shouted.

"What are you doing, Robbie?" she screamed. "You don't have a license!"

Robbie looked panic-stricken. "Quick!"

Jennifer glanced back over her shoulder. The Marines had cleared the line of cars and were closing in fast. She opened the driver's side door.

"Move over!" she ordered, climbing inside. "I'm driving."

Robbie resisted. "What are you talking about?"

"Your feet barely reach the pedal," she said. "Move! Now!"

She pushed Robbie into the passenger seat, closed her door, slipped behind the wheel and hit the accelerator.

The minivan lurched backward, knocking the front corner of a sedan and kicking up slush into the windshields of the cars behind it.

"Dang," she said.

"Dang?!" Robbie repeated, apoplectic.

She checked the rearview mirror and saw one of the Marines aiming his M-16 at them.

"Holy shit!" Robbie shouted. "They're going to shoot!"

Jennifer shifted into drive and they shot off.

She took the first corner too fast, and they slid across the ice, side-swiping a Jeep before gaining traction. Robbie slammed against the inside of the passenger door.

"What the hell did your mom do?" Robbie cried out.

"I don't know." Jennifer looked up in her rearview mirror, worried that bullets would shatter the back windshield at any moment. "But I'm not gonna sit around to find out."

She hit the accelerator again, and they sped off onto the straightaway.

CHAPTER EIGHTEEN

1210 Hours
Black Hawk One

It long before the chopper was skimming the white trees of the Hudson Valley and Sachs could see the hills of White Plains rising ahead. They must be going to the local airport. She thought of Jennifer on the run from the very people sent to help her, and worried that in her haste her daughter would put herself in harm's way.

"Where are you taking me?" she demanded.

Colonel Kyle of the Green Berets said nothing, but Special Agent Raghav of the Secret Service told her, "Nearest presidential emergency facility."

"Emergency?" Her brushes in the past with Washington security types had taught her a general rule of thumb: the less the inflection in the monotone voice, the worse the situation. "What kind of emergency?"

"There was an explosion in Washington a few minutes ago."

My God, she thought, I was supposed to be there tonight for the State of the Union address. Her mind raced through the multiple-choice scenarios. She closed her eyes and said, "Tell me the worst."

"It was nuclear."

The correct answer was: d) worse than she had imagined. Sachs snapped her eyes open and stared at the deadpan Secret Service agent. "How many casualties?" she heard herself ask hoarsely.

Raghav said, "Less than four thousand."

Sachs blinked. She could feel her throat catch. "That's how many died?"

"So far," Raghav said matter-of-factly. "The National Weather Service hasn't given us any updates on wind shifts. And fires are still burning. Should have been more than a million dead. But snow kept hundreds of thousands of federal workers home. And the nuke was small and exploded underground. Very clean. Minimal damage to civilians, maximum destruction to the federal government. Total decapitation."

"Decapitation," Sachs repeated, unsure what the jargon meant, although she had an idea. She suddenly felt lightheaded, her heart thumping beyond control. "Terrorists?"

"Nobody's claimed responsibility," Raghav said. "We think it's connected to what's happening in the Far East."

"Where's the president?"

"Dead."

Sachs took a deep breath. "And the vice president?"

"She's dead too."

"And the Speaker of the House?"

"They're all dead, ma'am," Raghav informed her. "Any designated presidential successors are being taken to secure facilities."

Sachs leaned back in her seat and stared out the window. America was at war, its leadership attacked. And Jennifer, her baby, was on the run. Sachs wanted to go back for her. But the hardened faces of the agents and Green Berets told her there was no turning back now.

Sachs asked, "So how many designated successors are there?"

Raghav was evasive. "I can't say for sure, ma'am."

"Something like fifteen or sixteen?"

Sachs suddenly felt something cold touch her temple. The barrel of an M4 came into view.

Pointing it at her was a grim Colonel Kyle with hate-filled eyes.

"One too many," he told her.

CHAPTER NINETEEN

1225 Hours
Nightwatch

Colonel Kozlowski looked around the conference table. The empty chairs were for the president and his staff. The secretary of defense. The national security adviser. Anybody else who survived, of which there was none.

What's wrong with this picture?

Koz sat alone at the head of the table and stared at a wall of display screens. The displays showed that American bombers were en route to their positive control points outside the Far East, where they would circle until they received further orders from the president-designate. Other displays showed that American submarine and missile crews were also awaiting executive authorization.

The only problem was that there was no president-designate to issue the launch authorizations. For that, Koz needed Deborah Sachs, of all people.

Northern Command's confirmation that Washington was gone—and with it Sherry--was devastating enough. Upon learning the news, Koz proceeded to spend several private minutes in the presidential bathroom throwing up the cold breakfast Sherry left for him.

Now the FEMA Central Locator confirmed that the SecDef was not at Edwards AFB in California after all but in Washington. Which meant he was dead and the presidential mantle had fallen to nearly last-in-line Deborah Sachs.

So Koz had ordered a change in course. Nightwatch was now en route to its rendezvous with the president-designate at an as-yet-undamaged airfield, in this case the local airport in White Plains, which had one runway barely long enough to handle an emergency 747 landing.

President Sachs. It just didn't sound right. "Madame President" would be the protocol. Unless she preferred Ms. President. Koz cringed at the thought.

Whatever his private opinions of the woman, Koz knew he had sworn an oath to protect and defend the

United States Constitution, and right now that meant Deborah Sachs.

The red phone next to his seat rang. He picked up. It was Captain Li. "We're cleared for approach," she said.

"Fine."

"And we've got footage from ground zero."

"I'll be right there."

He hung up, left the empty conference room and walked into the battle staff compartment where fifteen of his officers huddled around their monitors.

A traffic chopper from a Baltimore TV station was offering the world its first look at what had really happened in Washington, D.C.

Koz took a deep breath and looked over his crew. All eyes were glued to their monitors as the chopper was fast approaching a ridge of black trees.

"This is Chopper Dave," the traffic reporter pilot radioed from the cockpit. "Approaching ground zero."

Koz shook his head. Unless Chopper Dave's ride was shielded for radiation like Nightwatch, the traffic reporter was filing the last story of his life.

Chopper Dave was soaring over the ridge when suddenly there was...

Nothing.

A flat wasteland rolling on beneath gray skies.

Koz felt a pain in his stomach, like a knife had gone clean through, in and out.

"Oh, God."

He thought of Sherry, and realized she may have earned that Purple Heart after all. At the moment of impact she was probably sitting in her chair in Senator Vanderhall's office in the Hart Building, scripting some stupid sound bites for the self-important ass to parrot in reaction to the president's State of the Union address. Little did any of them know that a new president was going to have to address the fact that the state of the Union was cloudy with a chance of acid rain.

The monitors in the battle staff compartment displayed what Chopper Dave saw: devastation beyond recognition. Heaps of rubble, once buildings, lay scattered across the parched earth. A dark, snakelike fork was all that was left of the Potomac River. Radioactive fallout had already settled along its banks. Sporadic fires and black smoke completed a portrait straight out of Dante's *Inferno*.

"I'm circling the capitol." Chopper Dave's voice crackled over the intercom. Koz wasn't sure if it was the traffic reporter's voice or the reception breaking up. "No survivors in the impact area. Repeat. No survivors. At least none that we can see."

The battle staffers were watching the images, offering guesses as to the landmarks. "That stump is the Washington monument!" gasped one, pointing. "There!"

Koz wasn't sure. But the location looked right. His trance was broken when Captain Li came into the compartment to apologize for the bumpy landing.

"I didn't even know we touched down," Koz said.

The Nightwatch plane taxied to a stop along the runway. Hydraulic steps unfurled from the belly of the plane, and Koz descended to the tarmac where federal agents and vehicles were waiting.

"Where's the president-designate?" Koz demanded.

The special agent in charge, clearly a greenhorn from the bench, threw up his hands. "God knows, Colonel. Our boys called in to say she was picked up by two Black Hawks fifteen minutes ago."

"Should have been here by now," said Koz as he searched the dark skies in vain. He felt like some schmuck waiting for his blind date, fearing she was standing him up.

Captain Li, who had been standing at attention beside Koz, tugged his elbow. "Sir," she whispered. "We're vulnerable on the ground. I suggest we take off and continue to circle, or we're going to look like those images we just saw on TV after the next strike."

She was right, Koz realized, although he didn't want to leave. Finally, he said, "Tell De Carlo to keep the engines hot and prepare for take-off."

"Yes, sir," Li said.

"Tell him we'll circle for ten minutes," Koz said. "Then we follow the predesignated flight path out of the United States and proceed to the territory of an unattacked ally in the Southern Hemisphere."

"We're going south?"

Koz nodded. "Fallout free."

CHAPTER TWENTY

1230 Hours

Black Hawk One

W hat are you doing?!" Sachs stared at Colonel Kyle's M4.

Special Agent Raghav, meanwhile, put up his empty hands even as the young Secret Service agent next to him reached for his P90.

"I wouldn't do that," Kyle warned, and struck the agent's head with the butt of his M4. There was a sickening crack, and the agent collapsed to the floor.

"You crushed his skull!" Raghav yelled as another Green Beret expertly relieved him of his weapon.

Sachs looked down at the boy's body. The sight of hair matted in blood sickened her. "Why?"

"Ours is not to reason why, Ms. Sachs," Kyle replied, sliding open the Black Hawk's door. A blast of freezing air whooshed in, and Sachs found herself staring at the treetops below. "It's a tragic thing when accidents happen on military craft."

Sachs turned to Raghav and said, "Tell me you only look like a Secret Service agent. You're really an ex-SEAL or martial arts expert or something."

"I'm an ex-law student with a G-4 salary grade at the Treasury Department, ma'am," Raghav replied.

"Shut up!" Kyle kicked Raghav in the groin.

Raghav dropped to his knees in agony and moaned. Sachs saw Kyle swing the butt of his M4 across Raghav's face, knocking him to the floor, unconscious. Then he trained his machine gun on her. "On your knees."

"No," Sachs said. "I will not submit to your animal brutality and disregard for life, whatever the damn national security."

Kyle grabbed her by the hair. She struggled as he forced her down, choking back her urge to scream. "Think about what you're doing!"

"I'm thinking how I didn't serve my country to see it fall into the hands of a woman who was supposed to be fired today."

As Kyle put his M4 to her head, Raghav stirred to life and lunged at Kyle's jumpboots. Kyle lowered his M4 to fire, but Raghav pulled him off his feet.

Kyle's M4 spat out its automatic rounds. The bullets caught two Green Berets in the throat and drilled holes through the ceiling, making a sweeping arc of destruction over Kyle's falling body until they finally popped the pilot behind him.

The Black Hawk started to pitch and roll. The rest of Kyle's Green Berets were thrown back. Raghav grabbed Kyle's M4, turned and unloaded a round into the rear compartment before the Green Berets could recover. Fire shot out of the muzzle as Raghav jerked the trigger, raining dozens of smoking shells around Sachs, who was sprawled on the floor, hands clapped over her ears.

Suddenly, the shooting stopped. Sachs could hear only the rotor of the Black Hawk's blades and the howling wind. Or was that ringing in her ears?

"Are you OK?" asked Raghav, helping her up.

Sachs looked across the floor at the bodies and blood. Raghav impressed, after all. But she felt something awful rising up inside her, grabbed her stomach and started to heave.

Raghav gave her a helpful pat on the back and looked around. "Guess they took you for a liberal."

The Black Hawk banked sharply. Sachs turned to see the pilot slumped over in his seat.

"Oh, God."

Raghav climbed over the seat, pushing the pilot's body aside. He then took the controls and tried to level off.

Sachs climbed into the seat next to Raghav. "I suppose you can't fly, either?"

"No, ma'am."

"Then let me."

"You can't fly," Raghav said incredulously.

"No, but I watched my husband fly his planes, and I probably have more hours in the air than you do."

Raghav hesitated, and then the radio headset crackled. It was the pilot from Black Hawk Two. "Black Hawk One, you're trailing smoke."

Sachs watched Raghav struggle with the stick. It was a miracle they were still airborne. "If you or I respond, he's going to know Kyle's out," she said. "What's he going to do then?"

"Shoot us down if he's in with Kyle, or help us land if he's not. But we can't take a chance."

Sachs watched Raghav flick a switch to arm the Sidewinder missiles and stopped him. "You can't even pilot this thing, and you're going to try and down that chopper with your own men on board?"

"You are the priority, ma'am, and they know it."

The radio crackled again. "Black Hawk One, please copy."

"They're locking missiles on us," Raghav said, looking at the dashboard.

Sachs said, "Radio your men, Raghav, and tell them to take over that chopper. Now."

Raghav nodded and spoke into his lapel microphone. "Do not reply. Repeat. Do not reply. This is a Code 33. You have to take over that bird. Repeat. Code 33."

Sachs looked out at the Black Hawk behind them and to the left. It suddenly dipped as she saw a flurry of shadows inside. Then its cannons exploded. Sachs and Raghav jumped in their seats as 18 rounds of fire per second chewed holes around them.

"They've opened fire!" Raghav shouted.

"I can see that!"

Raghav said nothing, and Sachs felt a shiver up her spine. She glanced over at Raghav next to her and with a shock realized the handle of a knife was protruding from his neck. Her eyes widened as a bloody, monstrous Colonel Kyle reared his ugly head from behind and removed the red-stained blade.

"You'll never get sworn in," Kyle said, as he thrust the blade at her.

Sachs leaned away, escaping the first thrust. But she collided with Raghav's body and it fell on the stick, letting loose a burst of cannon fire. The chopper banked sharply, throwing Kyle off balance and sending her head into the windshield.

Dazed, she dragged herself forward and looked up to see Black Hawk Two smoking and spiraling out of control. For a moment, she saw what looked like a fight for control inside the cockpit before it went down and exploded in a ball of fire.

Sachs tried to crawl into the pilot's seat of her own chopper to avoid a similar fate. She had just about pushed Raghav's body out of the way when she felt a tug at her legs and looked back to see the bloody face of Colonel Kyle come to drag her back to hell.

"Get off me!" she screamed and kicked him in the face, her high heel spiking his eye.

Kyle loosened his grip and slid back limply as the chopper started to dive.

Sachs gripped the back of Raghav's bloody head, hoisted herself up on top of him and grabbed the stick. She saw the runway of the White Plains airport ahead.

She wiped her wet eyes and took a deep breath. The ground was coming up fast in the windshield, and the chopper began to spin with its own cloud of black smoke, going wobbly as it approached the small airport.

Sachs peered through the cracked windshield, straining to see. Then the curtain of smoke parted for a moment and she could see a team of federal agents and their vehicles waiting on the icy tarmac. A gigantic white jumbo jet dominated the runway.

She strapped herself into the pilot's chair, so tight she could barely steer. Everything seemed to be whooshing around her, and she felt her stomach drop with the chopper. She could see several Air Force personnel rushing toward her as she plunked the chopper down with a heavy thud. Then something seemed to give way as the chopper tipped over on its side and everything went black.

CHAPTER TWENTY-ONE

1315 Hours
Nightwatch

Colonel Kozlowski studied Sachs as she lay on the fold-out surgical table in the Nightwatch plane's medical center. Her eyes were closed beneath the high-intensity lights, an IV attached to her arm. Her black hair was brushed back from her face, her shoes removed and the belt around her skirt loosened.

The young medic had finished stitching a gash on her shoulder and was studying her with awe. Her bloody blouse was gone, and he gazed at the size C cups of her bra rising and falling as she breathed. He let out a low whistle. "Hail to the Chief."

"It's president-designate, Lieutenant Nordquist," said Koz, feigning indifference. "Nothing official until I know she's fit for office. Is she fit?"

"She's in better shape than those Green Berets on that Black Hawk, that's for sure." Nordquist started tapping up a chart for her on his tablet computer. "What the hell was that all about, anyway?"

That's what Koz wanted to know. What kind of remarkable woman could survive that kind of battle? Or cause it?

"You tell me," said Sachs, opening her eyes.

They were soft and brown, Koz noticed, but her voice was dry and cracked. It was probably the cabin air. He wondered how much she had heard. "Dehydration, ma'am."

"There's got to be a better explanation for their behavior than a lack of electrolytes."

"A dry wit too, thought Koz.

"No, ma'am. You're the one dehydrated. We'll give the IV another 20 minutes and take you off when we're at cruising altitude."

She started. "You mean we're in the air?"

"Thirty thousand feet," said Koz. "Welcome aboard the presidential Advanced Airborne Command Post."

"Then I want to see the president," she demanded, and Koz didn't know if she seriously didn't understand the situation or was testing him.

He paused. "Why?"

"Because those soldiers sent to pick me up tried to kill me," she said.

Koz blinked. "The Army Green Berets?"

She nodded. "Who sent them?"

"Uh, I did." He saw her eyes widen. "But I can assure you that I did not give Colonel Kyle orders to harm you or anyone else. He must have gone rogue."

She looked at him with a glint of paranoia. "Don't insult me with a lone gunman theory. Because he had a dozen others with him, all wearing the uniform of this country."

Koz exchanged a glance with Nordquist. "Physically, she checks outs," the medic said with a shrug. "Mentally, who knows? She's pretty shaken up."

"I'm fine," she said flatly. "Where's Special Agent Raghav?"

"Didn't make it, ma'am."

Her shoulders slumped and she dropped her head. "He was brave." Then her head snapped up again. "Jennifer," she said with a start, and swung her badly bruised and cut legs over the side of the table. "I want to talk to my daughter right now."

She tried to stand up, but a wave of dizziness seemed to pass over her and she started to sway.

Koz put a hand on her shoulder and braced her. "Easy now. I'm sure she's been taken care of."

"Like your Green Berets tried to take care of me?" she shot back.

"We'll find her, ma'am, I promise, and make sure she's safe."

"You do that, Colonel," she said, then noticed she had on nothing but a bra above her waist. She folded her arms over her chest, wincing as her shoulder flexed. "May I have my blouse back?"

"Try this." Koz opened a locker closet and pulled out an Air Force bomber jacket. He draped it over her shoulders.

"Thank you," she said with a shiver.

A beeping sounded in the medical compartment. Sachs jolted, turning to see if it was one of her medical monitors. But Koz walked over to the intercom on the wall and punched a button. "What is it?"

Captain Li's voice squawked over the speaker: "Sir, we have NCA commanders on screen for the attack conference."

"I'll be right there," he replied, and turned to leave.

"You're just going to leave me here?" Sachs demanded. "I don't think so." She took two steps and was restrained by her IV feeds like a dog on its leash. "I demand you take me to see the president, Colonel Kozlowski, even if she's in the mirror."

Kozlowski looked back at her without answering her implicit claim, although he felt a pang of guilt mixed with uncertainty. "I think it's best that you're confined to these quarters pending a thorough medical review."

"Are you serious, Colonel?" Her tired, brown eyes seemed to search his face and heart for something Koz felt was no longer there.

Koz gave a cool nod to Nordquist, who was already preparing a syringe. "We want to avoid any panic until our forces are in place."

"What the hell is that supposed to mean?" Sachs shouted as Koz put his hand on the door.

"Trust me, it's for your own good," he said, and walked out.

An alarmed Captain Li was waiting for him in the hallway as the door slid shut behind him like a coffin on a protesting Sachs and syringe-wielding Nordquist.

"Where is she?" Li asked as he brushed past her toward the battle staff compartment. "What's going on in there?"

He said, "She's recuperating."

Li was on his heels like a terrier. "Recuperating? Hello? Are we back in the USSR or what?"

"Can it," he said as he marched into the next compartment.

Li would not let up, nor would he expect her to. "She *is* our only legal president, and our respect for a higher authority, in this case the Constitution, is the only thing that separates us from the boys in Beijing."

Koz nodded as they entered the battle staff compartment. "Let me feel out the others on the conference call."

"You're talking about a coup, sir."

Koz caught a few stray glances from the young crew as they passed by. *A little louder, Li,* he thought.

"She's delirious, Captain," he told her, waiting until they had entered the empty briefing room. "She accused me of trying to kill her. How much credibility is she going to have with her commanders if she starts making wild claims like that? You really want her in charge?"

"What I want and what is right are often two different things, sir."

"Let me put this another way, Captain." He turned to face her, square on. "America has just suffered its worst military attack in history. We're on the brink of universal Armageddon. As president, Deborah Sachs is not some civilian politician but our commander-in-chief. Would you follow this woman into battle?"

Her answer was firm and unwavering. "Yes, I would."

Koz studied Li's stoic, determined face. "Well, I'm not so sure."

Li simply stood there, not giving in.

Koz took a breath. "OK," he told her. "While I speak to the NCA, I want you to check whatever DOD records we have left and see if this guy Kyle has a history with anybody who could have given orders to kill Sachs. But discreetly."

"Yes, sir."

He could see the approval in her face.

"And while you're at it," Koz said, "check out the last communications between the White House and Pentagon. Check anything unusual that happened in the city within the past two or three days. Everything should have been backed up at remote DOD servers before the blast."

"Yes, sir. Anything else?"

"Find Jennifer Sachs."

Koz sat down at the head of an empty conference table and looked up at the big screen on the wall, wondering how exactly he was going to explain Deborah Sachs.

CHAPTER TWENTY-TWO

1316 Hours
Nightwatch

Inside the Nightwatch infirmary, Sachs recoiled as Nordquist flicked the long needle of a syringe with his finger until some clear liquid spurted out. "Don't worry, ma'am," he said as he approached her with the hypodermic. "You'll feel a lot better after this."

She braced herself against the edge of the surgical table. "Lieutenant, there is no way in hell that you're going to drug me with whatever is in that thing."

"Propofol," he said, reaching for her arm. "A sedative-hypnotic drug to put you to sleep. It's terrific. No side effects like hangover or nausea. Trust me, you'll feel a lot better when you wake up."

She leaned against the surgical table, trying to escape his grasp.

"This is for your own good, ma'am," he said, trying to jab her.

She arched over the table until she was almost on her back. But before he could take another swipe, she leaned back in a rocking motion, lifting her legs and then shoving both feet into his gut, pushing him back against the opposite wall. His head slammed against a cabinet and he dropped to the floor, writhing in pain.

She jumped off the table and grabbed the hypodermic he had dropped on the floor. He was trying to get back on his feet, and she couldn't let him, or he'd overpower her. With a quick thrust she plunged the needle into his neck before he slapped her away.

He began to sway back and forth, even as he shook his head at her.

"That wasn't nice," he said and then collapsed into her arms.

"Your medicine, doc," she said, barely able to hold up his weight. She eased him down to the floor, where he lay unconscious.

As she stood up, she felt a terrific pain in her shoulder. The regional anesthetic was starting to wear off. Somehow she managed to put her bloody blouse back on and surveyed the room: three first-class seats, two bunk beds, a sink, a refrigerator for blood and medicines and a closet full of medical equipment.

Outside the compartment, beyond locked doors, were more of Koz's crew. So she was going nowhere. Not at thirty thousand feet.

She had a hard time believing Kozlowski could be in on this. He was a uniform like General Marshall and Colonel Kyle. But the way he touched her face with his hand—it was warm and caring, like Richard's. His actions, however, seemed to have proven otherwise.

Perhaps he would say the same of her, what with that chopper business and now knocking out the good doctor. But this was self-defense, she determined as she looked down at the medic. And the odds were horribly uneven—one woman in a plane filled with trained soldiers. All she had on her side were a couple of visits to Jennifer's Wing-Chun Kung Fu class. She picked up no moves, only the idea to use anything available to strike back at your enemy, even his own weapons.

In this case, it was the doc's own hypodermic.

She checked Nordquist on the floor. He was completely out, but the angle of his body seemed uncomfortable. The least she could do was slip a pillow under his head.

She began to search for one and then saw her purse on a counter. Her cell phone was still inside. She wondered if it would actually work, and, if it did, if anyone would answer. She desperately wanted to talk to Jennifer and her sister Dina, find out if they were OK, tell them she was fine. Which she wasn't.

She picked up the purse, pulled out her phone and pressed the #2 key to dial Jennifer's number.

CHAPTER TWENTY-THREE

1317 Hours
Bedford Hills

Jennifer turned the wheel hard, and the minivan skidded onto an unplowed country road. As she pulled at the steering wheel to adjust, her phone started ringing. She tightened one hand on the wheel and with the other dug into the front pocket of her jeans for her phone. But Robbie tried to stop her.

"You still have your phone?" he shrieked. "Don't answer it! They can track us!"

But Jennifer's hand was already around her phone and pulled it out. The display showed "The Deb" and her mother's number. She answered. "Mom, where are you?"

"Thank God you're OK." It was her mom's voice, but the connection wasn't good at all. Her phone showed five bars for reception, but her mom sounded like she was a mile underground. "Listen, Jennifer. Those men chasing you."

"Don't tell me they're just trying to help, Mom."

"No, Jennifer. They want to hurt you."

Jennifer felt a shiver up her spine and involuntarily swerved the minivan around the next corner. "What?"

"They want…"

"You're cutting out, Mom."

Jennifer, trying to drive and talk, turned onto another road and saw a Westchester County Sheriff's highway patrol car coming their way. She held her breath as they passed each other, then looked up in the mirror to see the patrol car make a long, sloppy U-turn in the snow.

"They found us!" she shouted into her phone.

"Jennifer!" Her mom's voice rang out.

Robbie was screaming hysterically, "Get rid of the fricking phone!"

Jennifer lowered her window, tossed the phone into the snow and drove away as fast as she could from the flashing lights behind her.

"We're screwed," Robbie said. "There's no way we're going to outrun the cops."

She had enough and slowed down.

"What are you doing?" Robbie shouted.

"Kicking you out of the van."

"Shut up and drive!"

"You shut up, Robbie, and then I'll drive."

He finally chilled out and she looked up in her mirror in time to see the police car get rammed by a black Suburban. The Suburban pummeled the police car into an icy wall of plowed snow, then began to back up and ram it again and kill the driver. She could see two Green Berets inside the Suburban.

"Holy crap!" she screamed and hit the accelerator.

The minivan skidded forward until it got its grip on the ice, and she slowly applied more pressure to speed away. She made several sharp turns through the maze of winding winter roads, losing sight of the Suburban behind her and praying against reason that the goons behind the wheel wouldn't pick up her trail.

CHAPTER TWENTY-FOUR

1318 Hours
Nightwatch

Three puzzled faces stared at Koz from their respective screens inside the Nightwatch conference compartment: General Block at Northern Command, General Carver at STRATCOM and General Marshall aboard the Looking Glass Airborne Command.

Carver in Omaha was the first to speak. "What the hell do you mean she's incapacitated, Colonel?"

"Just that, sir," Koz replied, learning forward in his seat at the end of the long, empty conference table. "She got pretty banged up when her chopper went down en route to the designated rendezvous." Koz watched the generals closely for any reaction. "She said the Green Beret escort I sent tried to kill her."

Block's round face turned beet red. "Lord Almighty!" he said. "What do the Green Berets say?"

"Nothing, sir. They're all dead."

Koz thought he caught a tick at the corner of Block's left eye, but he couldn't be sure.

"Colonel, are you trying to tell us that this…woman…single-handedly took out an entire Green Beret escort in two choppers?"

It did sound unbelievable, Koz realized, the way Block put it. "She had the help of her Secret Service detail, none of whom survived."

"How convenient," Block muttered. "For all we know, Sachs is the one taking orders and the Chinese wanted her to be president."

There was silence. Absolute silence. Koz stared at the screens, waiting for the first sign of an emotion to cross any one of the three faces. It was a ballsy, completely out-there accusation from Block, but something they had to chew on.

"We all know how the chain of command works in a situation like this," Marshall explained, breaking the silence. "The National Command Authority is in charge of our nuclear forces. In peacetime, that's usually the president and the secretary of defense. In time of war, it's their designated successors and us, the surviving commanders. As things now stand, the president is only one voice out of four. And in military matters, she'd obviously defer to us. But politically—constitutionally—we still need presidential authorization, and that requires a president. That president, for better or worse, is Deborah Sachs."

More silence. Koz could sense both Carver and Block almost wishing Marshall to put up his hand for the job himself. He had earned it, Koz knew, that's for sure. His deference to the Constitution only confirmed his leadership ability in time of war.

"Marshall's right," Carver concluded, his tone signaling that he was bringing the first attack conference to a close. "The last thing we need is a constitutional crisis. America can't go into this war split. I think Sachs could work. She has to work. She will review the attack options while we move our forces into place. Then, when the time comes, Colonel Kozlowski can relay her strike authorization. If Marshall is right, she'll play ball."

"Play ball?" Block repeated incredulously. "How the hell do you expect her to play ball, boys, if she ain't got none?"

Koz opened his mouth to offer his own observation when his comlink beeped. It was Captain Li. "Sir, we have an unauthorized, outbound transmission originating from the medical center," she reported. "The officers on duty outside can't break in. The door is jammed."

Sachs.

Koz said, "I'll be right there."

CHAPTER TWENTY-FIVE

1319 Hours

Sachs texted her daughter from inside the infirmary of the Nightwatch plane: *J, where r u?* But Jennifer wasn't responding. She tried calling again, at least getting a ring this time. She waited for what seemed like an eternity when Jennifer's voicemail message came through. "Say what you gotta say and leave me alone, loser."

"Jennifer, it's mom," she said, trying to sound calm but forceful. "You know what's going on with the attack. I have to know where you are and that you're safe. We need to stay connected. Call or text me back right away."

Knowing Jennifer, she was probably heading home to Dina's, which would be the first place anybody pursuing her would be waiting.

"Don't go to Aunt Dina's," Sachs pleaded into the phone, then said it again quietly. "Don't go anywhere near the house."

Sachs hung up and paced back and forth in the medical center, deciding what to do next. She tried all of Dina's numbers, getting only voicemails or service interruption messages. She had to reach somebody on the outside, someone in government or media, she decided, to let them know where she was and find out what was going on in the outside world. Someone beyond the D.C.-New York beltway. Maybe California. Rhinehart's former press secretary, Vicki Blaze, was the news manager at NBC in Los Angeles. She might even put the call live on the air right there and then. Assuming NBC was still on the air on the West Coast.

She typed in Vicki's name on her phone to call up the number and was about to hit "dial" when Colonel Kozlowski burst through the door with Captain Li and two armed Nightwatch officers.

Sachs froze as Li rushed over to Nordquist slumped on the floor. "He's unconscious, sir."

Kozlowski gave her a wild look and pointed an accusing finger at her phone. "Did you just make an unauthorized call?"

Before she could answer, he grabbed the phone and waved it in her face. "Our flight plan is secret!"

His face was red with fury, the gentle touch gone. Somehow she was the enemy again. "You've compromised our location to anybody listening! Enemy missiles could get a lock on us because of your stupidity!"

He was shouting at her now. Her ears hurt.

"Listen, Colonel," she replied calmly, the way she whispered to a rowdy classroom so the kids had to shut up to hear her. "I'm having a tough time getting up to speed on my new responsibilities. No thanks to the medication you gave me. I'd appreciate it if you treated me with a little respect and were kinder and gentler."

Koz looked at her like she was from another planet. "Gentler?" he repeated. "This isn't the Hallmark Channel. This isn't about you being a symbol of plucky feminism making her mark in a male-dominated world. This is war. You think the enemy is going to be gentle on you?"

"No," Sachs replied, "but I expect my friends to be. Are you my friend, or are you my enemy, Colonel?"

Her words seemed to have an effect on him. He was looking at her as a real woman now, not some anonymous civilian. He seemed to be aware of the gravity of his verbal assault, because his tough facade began to melt.

"Yes, ma'am."

"Am I or am I not the designated president of the United States?"

Koz, aware of his officers, slowly nodded. "You are, Madame President, as soon as we swear you in."

"And you have sworn an oath to defend the Constitution of the United States?"

"Yes, ma'am."

"I may not be everybody's idea of a president, much less a commander-in-chief," she told them. "But I used to teach American History. And the history of America taught me that right is stronger than might. Right now, the U.S. Constitution has decided that there is only one right person for this job, and that person happens to be me. If we stay on the right side of history here, we will win."

She looked into the eyes of the young crew members. Some seemed barely older than the middle and high school students she once taught. Only Koz, with his weathered face, looked like a battle-scarred survivor of previous wars. She watched their heads nod, acknowledging her appeal to their moral conscience, deeply impressing her.

"Now may I please confer with my military commanders?" She fixed her gaze squarely on Koz. "Before we waste any more time?"

"Yes, ma'am. But first the Constitution."

Koz glanced over at the disheveled medic being slapped into consciousness by Captain Li. "Nordquist, get up off the floor and fix those cuts on the president's face," he barked. "Li, go grab your Bible and a camera and some make-up. We need to release an official photo of the swearing-in."

Then Sachs watched his hazel eyes look into her own, look through them and deep into her.

"She seems fit to me," he declared. "Inform the pilots our call sign has changed to Air Force One."

CHAPTER TWENTY-SIX

1426 Hours
Bedford Hills

Jennifer turned the minivan up the long incline overlooking her aunt's grand 1890 carriage house that abutted the riding trails. The secluded home looked dark and foreboding. Inside the minivan, the radio was playing with continuous news reports from New York's WCBS-AM.

Jennifer pulled to a stop and looked out the frosty window at the house in the distance. It was early afternoon, but with the January snow it felt like early evening. She hadn't seen the Suburban for an hour, and she was tired of playing hide-and-seek. If they had hoped to find her here, they would have already come and gone.

Robbie, tense as ever, observed, "The lights are off."

"Doesn't mean anything," Jennifer said. "Carla likes to keep the ConEd bills low for my aunt when she's out of town. It's like a freezer inside."

"You mean your aunt isn't even home?"

"Vacation in the Bahamas with her boyfriend," Jennifer said. "But there's a loaded .357 Magnum locked up in a closet, food in the kitchen, and a place to hide in the basement."

The news on the radio was suddenly interrupted by a flat, ominous tone. A deep, authoritarian voice blared from the speaker.

"This is the Emergency Alert System. This is not a test. Repeating. This is not a test."

"Holy crap!" Robbie squeaked.

Jennifer looked at Robbie and suddenly wondered what she ever saw in this wus. "Shut up and listen." She turned up the volume.

"This is an Emergency Alert Message from the president of the United States."

But it wasn't President Rhinehart that came on. It was a woman.

"Whereas an unprovoked nuclear attack has been launched against the United States by foreign military forces…"

Jennifer listened closely to the distant but familiar voice.

"…And whereas the exigencies of the international situation and of the national defense require the suspension of traditional democratic practices…"

Jennifer cocked her ear in disbelief. "Mom?"

"We're doomed!" Robbie moaned.

Jennifer punched him in the arm. "I told you to shut up!"

"…Now therefore I, Deborah Sachs, president of the United States, hereby proclaim that a state of war exists."

Oh, my God, Jennifer thought, clapping both her frozen hands over her mouth.

Robbie pointed an accusing finger at the dashboard radio. "Hey, the Constitution says only Congress can declare war."

Jennifer cracked open her door and planted one boot in the snow.

"Hey!" Robbie shouted. "Where are you going?"

"Are you deaf?" she said. "Didn't you just hear the radio? My mom and Aunt Dina are probably worried sick about me. I can call them from inside the house and let them know I'm OK. You coming?"

"No way," he said and slid behind the wheel. He quickly adjusted the driver's seat so his feet could reach the pedals. "You're surrendering."

"I'm the First Kid now," she told him. "Everybody has to listen to me. Including you. Fine, drive home to your folks. They're probably just as worried."

She shut the door and watched him put the minivan into reverse, back up and then screech down the road, disappearing into the darkening afternoon. She turned and trudged through the knee-high snow down the hillside, one long stride after another, toward Aunt Dina's house.

She burst through the front door, key in hand. "Carla? Carla?" she called for the housekeeper.

The living room, filled with expensive built-ins and antiques and period rugs, was empty. "Carla?" she called out, then ran up the stairs to the bedrooms.

But the bedrooms were empty too, including her own. She looked at the shelves next to her bed lined with trophies from soccer, basketball and softball. Even the trophies, however, were dwarfed by the ribbons and cups from her horse-riding conquests. But it was the solid crystal cube— a commemorative urn—on the middle shelf that caught her eye. Etched in the crystal was an outline of an old-fashioned biplane and the words:

Richard Sachs
1975 – 2011

Jennifer looked at it for a long moment, then turned and walked into the hallway again, calling Carla's name.

Maybe Carla left, she thought as she hurried down the stairs and ran into the kitchen, tripping over a pile of laundry. She landed hard and sprawled across the floor.

"Owww," she cried out.

She pushed up with her hands to get on all fours when she saw the blood on the travertine tiles and froze. Slowly she willed her eyes to follow the blood trail until it ended at Carla's skull.

"Oh, my God!" she screamed and jumped back.

Carla was on her back, staring at the ceiling, a small, dark hole in her forehead. Jennifer glanced up at the window over the sink. There was a hole in the center of a spider-web crack.

A sniper got Carla, she realized, feeling her heart pounding out of her chest as she gasped for air. *Somebody's out there.*

She didn't dare stand up again. Instead she crawled along the cabinetry and poked her head around the corner to look outside the sliding glass door. A black Suburban suddenly hit its high beams, blinding her. She recoiled and crouched back behind the counter.

"No, no, no," she moaned.

She peeked out again and saw the silhouettes of two shadowy figures with guns—M4s from the profiles—walking toward the house.

She ducked back out of sight, staring at Carla on the floor in front of her. Warm tears rolled down her frozen cheeks as she bit down hard on her lower lip.

Her mom was right.

CHAPTER TWENTY-SEVEN

1431 Hours
Air Force One

Inside the presidential bathroom of the Nightwatch plane, now officially Air Force One, Sachs wiped off the makeup Captain Li had applied for the swearing-in photo and looked at herself in the mirror. Other than the bruises on her forehead, she didn't look too banged up. But she also didn't look like an American president, she thought, and she certainly didn't feel like one. As if to underscore her testosterone deficit, she caught a glimpse of the prominent urinal behind her in the mirror.

She zipped up the flightsuit Captain Li had given her—presidential seal and all—and walked out into the presidential suite. It was a smaller compartment than she had imagined, dominated by a desk, an

American flag and a long gold couch from which a grim Colonel Kozlowski and Captain Li rose as she entered.

Sachs said, "What's FEMA doing for the victims and their families in Washington, D.C.?"

"Everything humanly possible, Madame President," said Captain Li. "First-response medical units from around the country are treating the wounded and tagging the dead. Communications command posts are being set up to handle family inquiries. And financial credits are being applied to all affected."

Sachs then looked at Koz and said simply, "Jennifer."

"Soon as we've located her, we'll put you on with her, Madame President," Kozlowski assured her. "Meanwhile, Captain Li has General Zhang on behalf of the People's Republic of China on hold."

Sachs said, "What happened to President Peng Hu?"

Kozlowski shook his head. "China has made it clear that Zhang is their point man with us."

Not a good sign at all, Sachs thought.

She looked at the phone on the desk in front of her, light blinking. She sat down behind the desk. There was a presidential seal on the bulkhead above her left shoulder.

She swallowed hard and then nodded to Kozlowski, who pressed the speaker button.

"General Zhang," she said. "This is Deborah Sachs."

She heard a quick translation from Captain Li, then General Zhang's voice and another translation.

"The people of China wish to express our profound sorrow for your loss today, Madame President, and desire to offer any assistance the United States may require."

Sachs replied, "The only thing I require, General Zhang, is confirmation from your own lips that neither you nor any agent of the Chinese military was responsible for today's attack on Washington, D.C."

"We are not responsible," General Zhang said firmly. "But we will consider any retaliation directed at us an act of war. If so, I guarantee you that many other American cities shall suffer the same fate as Washington."

Before she could reply, Zhang hung up. She looked at Kozlowski. "Now what?"

"You'll review your options. The National Command Authority is waiting on screen in the conference room for your first attack conference. That's General Norman Block at Northern Command, General Duane Carver at Strategic

Command, and General Brad Marshall aboard our Looking Glass plane."

"Looking Glass?" she asked. "What's that?"

"An airborne command post like this plane, with a few additional military modifications thrown in," Kozlowski told her.

Brad Marshall, thought Sachs with mixed emotions. *She would be conferring with* the *Brad Marshall. Wouldn't Jennifer be impressed?*

General Brad Marshall did indeed impress from the moment she stepped into the conference center and saw him on the big screen. He was flanked by General Carver on the left and General Block on the right, who started things off with his own commentary on the D.C. strike.

"Charlie looks guilty as hell, Madame President," Block said, full of bluster.

Sachs said, "So I hear, General Block. And we know this because?"

General Carver, the ranking general of the three, said, "Marshall, you better tell her."

"Welcome, Madame President," Marshall began. "Have you ever heard of an online video game called Red Glare?" His voice was very smooth and inspired immediate credibility and confidence.

"I know what the Red Glare is." Sachs instinctively touched Jennifer's "Fembot Fiona"

USB flashdrive hanging from her neck. "But what does it have to do with the real world?

"A lot, actually," Marshall said. "The DOD has been closely monitoring this game for almost two years now, because it is the only program or application of any kind running on one of the Chinese military's newest Shuguang supercomputers. It's not public, but new Shuguang runs 50% faster than Japan's Fugaku and our own IBM Summit. So you've got the world's most powerful supercomputer running nothing but a video game."

Sachs was hooked. "Why would the Chinese give their most powerful computer system over to a video game?"

"Same reason the Chinese have been running other cloud-based games like Farmville and virtual worlds like Second Life on their next dozen most powerful supercomputers," Marshall said. "Red Glare is basically the world's eBay for arms dealers and terrorists."

"What?" Sachs blinked. "You lost me, General."

Marshall said, "Gamers around the world can buy or sell virtual goods or weapons with real money to help them advance to the next level in these games. Players end up spending more money on their virtual upgrades than they do buying the game itself, making the game companies—and the supercomputer's owners—billions."

Sachs nodded. She remembered the first time her credit cards showed charges from PayPal and Apple Pay for Jennifer's purchases of "accessories" like exploding diamond earrings and biotoxin-tipped fingernails for her Fembot Fiona avatar. The accessories were pure fantasy, but the money was real.

"I think I follow you now, General Marshall. What looks like a grenade launcher online for a player's avatar like Fembot Fiona or Duke Droid might actually represent a real grenade launcher—or a stolen Soviet SS-20 warhead. Is that it?"

Marshall seemed surprised at how quickly she put it together, but pleasantly so. "Exactly, Madame President."

Sachs didn't know if it was his surprise that bothered her or that his opinion mattered to her more than it should. "Monitoring an arms deal isn't the same as brokering the deals, much less being party to it," she said, pressing on. "How do we know for sure it was the Chinese who bought the SS-20 that exploded in Washington today?"

"Two things," Marshall said. "First, the former deputy Russian FSB intelligence chief and arms dealer who was trying to sell the SS-20 in South

Africa confessed under joint CIA-FSB interrogation. He said he sold it to an agent of the Chinese military. You can call up the video on your workstation aboard Nightwatch. Excuse me, Air Force One. The three warheads were placed on a Chinese freighter bound from Cape Town to Baltimore. The assembly of the housing and detonation devices took place in transit across the Atlantic."

She glanced down at the conference table and realized there was a computer screen beneath the surface playing the footage. When she placed her finger on the table a touchscreen keyboard terminal appeared.

So cool, she thought, *Jennifer would love this.* But she quickly pushed the thought away, along with her natural questions about what form of "interrogation" the CIA and FSB used on this arms dealer.

She asked Marshall, "So you're telling me there might be two more warheads out there?"

"Yes, ma'am."

She exhaled. "What's the second thing that fingers China as the state sponsor of this morning's nuke attack and this imminent Red Glare threat?"

"A cyberweapon that we eventually tracked back to China attacked Pentagon computers nine months ago," Marshall said. "At first, U.S. Cyber Command assumed it came from the Middle East, in retaliation for another nextgen Stuxnet worm the Israelis used to sabotage an Iranian nuclear power station."

"I remember," said Sachs, looking down at a report on her screen detailing the work of Unit 8200, the signal intelligence arm of the Israeli Defense Forces. "Something about a biblical reference to the Book of Esther that was embedded in the computer code. It pointed to Israel as the originator of the cyber attack. So there's something like that in the code of this cyberweapon that points to China?"

"Yes," Marshall said. "The Chinese characters for 'Red Glare.' This Red Glare cyberworm infiltrated our most critical systems. We haven't been able to get rid of it, and we don't know what its true purpose is, other than it's malicious."

Sachs asked, "What could it possibly do?"

"Well, just imagine America in another pandemic shutdown without Zoom video conferencing, Amazon eCommerce, Netflix streaming or any Internet access. Then consider what happens when ATMs can't spit out cash and millions can't tap their government stimulus checks. People would go crazy. Some literally within three days when they can't refill their antidepressants. What we consider rioting and looting in the streets is nothing compared to what happens then."

"Well, then why hasn't it happened yet?" she demanded. "What hasn't this Red Glare worm already taken down our physical infrastructure, including our power grids and defense systems?"

"We think it already has, in part," Marshall told her. "We've been waiting for the other shoe to drop. It did today with the attack on D.C. Or, more accurately, the nuke this morning was the first shoe. Now we're waiting for the second shoe to drop when Red Glare reveals its true nature."

Sachs pressed. "What is that nature, General Marshall? What exactly do you believe is the purpose of this Red Glare cyberweapon?"

"To degrade our ability to respond under attack, Madame President," Marshall said.

"Respond to what exactly, General?"

"An invasion of Taiwan, for starters. Possibly more nukes. My counterparts in Beijing have already publicly stated we'd never risk Los Angeles for Taipei."

"Actually, I know some people who would."

"Either way, China will dump all their Treasuries, bankrupt us and replace the U.S. dollar with the yuan as the world's reserve currency. Best case scenario, the U.S. would follow the British Empire into relative geopolitical and economic oblivion."

"Worst case?"

"We cease to exist. Or, more likely, we'd become a vassal state at the mercy of China's stranglehold of global supply chains. Not just tech but food and pharma. They could unleash another virus on us at any time from which we'd have no cure, no vaccine, and no means to manufacture any on our own. Our destiny would no longer belong to us. Google, Apple, Facebook and Amazon would be nothing more than satellites for the Chinese surveillance state. We'd be done. In some ways, we already are."

She knew he had been saying as much in the media in recent years. But she wasn't sure what he was telling her now. "What are you saying?"

"Madame President, the Chinese may already have the tech in place to take out our planes and missiles, even our satellites. We won't know for sure until they carry out their missions."

"What does that mean?" she asked.

"It means that if you don't act now, Madame President, you might not be able to act at all."

CHAPTER TWENTY-EIGHT

1435 Hours
Looking Glass

Marshall's first read on Sachs was that she had a much quicker grasp of an evolving situation than her predecessor Rhinehart. But he was worried about her trigger finger. He doubted she was born with one.

He sat back in his chair inside the battle staff compartment of his Looking Glass plane and studied President Sachs on the split screen as she took in everything he said. General Carver's expression from Omaha seemed to be giving her the benefit of the doubt. But then Carver was a consensus builder who only weighed in at the end after all viewpoints were shared.

General Block, buried under Cheyenne Mountain, looked like he was about to burst. Marshall saw it coming a full minute before Block opened his mouth. "Say the word, Madame President, and we're ready to point and shoot."

Marshall groaned inside and watched Sachs start.

"Point and shoot?" she repeated incredulously. "That's the option you're giving me?"

Marshall cleared his throat and addressed the screen. "You've basically have three decent options, Madame President," he told her. "Tall, Grande and Venti."

She seemed to bristle for a moment at his "mansplaining," although he'd used the same analogy before with President Rhinehart. "Venti, I suppose, means an all-out nuclear attack like General Block is suggesting?"

Marshall said, "Basically."

Sachs said, "I don't want to bring an end to China, gentlemen. I want to end this war before it gets out of control. So we can eliminate the Venti option right now. What's the so-called Grande option?"

"Limited strike," Marshall said. "We wipe out their artificial islands in the South China Sea. But we spare their most valued targets on the mainland and leave them at risk. That way the enemy has a strong incentive to seek an end to the conflict. As you just said, that's what we want: an end to the escalation."

"What if they don't 'get' that we're only inflicting limited harm? They're liable to launch everything they've got at us. What's the Tall option?"

Marshall didn't like the direction this conversation was going. "Something you can reliably recall, like our new B-21 stealth bomber. But instead of the usual thermonuclear weapons we arm it with a nuclear-tipped Maverick surface-penetrating cruise missile."

"A Maverick?"

"I'm sending the data over right now," Marshall said, and immediately a 3-D model appeared on the screen. "It's a next-generation bunker-buster that can burrow through hundreds of feet of earth and concrete and knock out Zhang's underground headquarters."

Sachs blinked. "You call that the 'tall' option?"

"Yes," Marshall said. "Just like they took out Washington. Tit for tat. An eye for an eye. An underground detonation means no fallout or wind shift worries and collateral civilian casualties. There's even a scenario in there that liberates China.

"Or their DF-5 missiles," said a voice off screen, and then Marshall saw Nightwatch's chief communications officer, Captain Linda Li, lean toward Sachs on screen and mumble something.

Marshall knew Li had a point, but it was obvious that Colonel Kozlowski, standing behind Sachs, didn't like it. Neither did Block or Carver onscreen. Neither did he. It was all he could do to not tempt the fates by reminding Sachs that if she and her kind hadn't scrapped his proposed Defender anti-ballistic system, this would be an entirely different conversation and her options would look a hell of a lot better than the box she was in now.

Sachs nodded on screen and then said, "Once battlefield nukes are used, it's too easy for both sides to justify using more destructive weapons. I'm not going to let it get that far."

"But it won't get that far, Madame President," Marshall injected, aware that his voice revealed the first sign of impatience with her. "Because our Mavericks will decapitate the entire Chinese C3I command-and-control structure. Just like they tried with us."

"Yes, and leave no Chinese government to negotiate a cease-fire or surrender."

"Not true," Marshall said. "The government of our ally Taiwan would replace the old regime, and Taipei would become the new capital of China."

"Assuming the Chinese don't invade Taiwan or destroy it first." She paused. "Something is wrong with this picture. I mean, why haven't our forward-deployed forces in the Far East been attacked?"

Block, who looked like he was going to burst a blood vessel this whole time, finally blurted out, "Who the hell cares? They hit D.C.! For the love of God, lady, make up your mind!"

She ignored the entire "woman-who-can't-make-up-her-mind" slur. "I need to think this over, before I make an irrevocable decision that could potentially kill millions of people."

Block could barely contain himself. "Think it over?" he cried. "Think it over? You're not supposed to think, Sachs. You're supposed to execute your duties as commander in chief."

General Carver, clearly sensing this so-called "attack conference" was coming to an unfavorable conclusion, seconded Block. "Not to decide is a decision in itself, Madame President."

"Let me be clear," she concluded. "For now, I refuse to escalate this conflict."

She cut out, leaving Marshall alone facing a blank screen with Quinn standing awkwardly next to him, embarrassed that anyone should speak to the Great American Defender this way.

Marshall simply shook his head and answered the screen, "And if the enemy escalates it?"

CHAPTER TWENTY-NINE

1436 Hours
Air Force One

Kozlowski stepped outside Sachs' compartment to give her "time to think," shut the door behind him and glared at Captain Li. "What the hell were you doing there, Li, spooking the president with visions of DF-5 nukes raining down on us? You and I have no opinions with regards to attack options."

"I was providing my commander-in-chief with potential consequences of her actions, like she asked." Li offered no apologies. "You think President Rhinehart would have given us the time of day if he were on board with his VP, SecDef and members of the NSC? History has appointed you and me as the new president's primary protectors and filters of information. Otherwise, Marshall and the NCA might as well be running the country."

"That may not be such a bad thing at this point, Captain." Koz looked at the presidential seal on the door dividing them from Sachs. "What the hell is she doing in there?"

"Maybe she's dancing to Taylor Swift. Or praying. Or bawling her eyes out. Who besides God needs to know?"

"I do, Captain. I need to know. I have no idea what Sachs is thinking. Only that she is. Doesn't that worry you?"

"A woman who thinks for herself?"

Koz stared at Li's black, penetrating eyes. "Of course not," he said, and then he held up the small action figure USB flashdrive Sachs had given him at his request and handed it to Li. "This belongs to Jennifer Sachs. Scan the files and see if there's any clue to where she might have gone."

"Wow, Fembot Fiona," Li remarked as she took the flashdrive. "I'll check her social media too. Instagram is down, but Tik Tok is still up. If she's not talking to her mom, she might be talking to friends."

CHAPTER THIRTY

1437 Hours
Bedford Hills

Jennifer crouched beneath the kitchen window of her Aunt Dina's house in terror, staring at Carla's body, aware of the red lasersights probing through the dark.

She crawled into the adjoining laundry room, rummaged through Carla's purse and found her phone. She dialed her mom's number. Then she heard a crash in the kitchen and froze.

They were in the house.

She could hear the soft, quick shuffles of their shoes fan out looking for her. She held her breath and looked around. Her only way out was through the dog door.

She glanced back in time to see a red laser target beam probe the kitchen. She pushed her body through the narrow door, wishing Aunt Dina's dog Admiral were here right now and not at the kennel. She was halfway out the door when her foot caught on the other side. She tried to shake it loose when she felt a gloved hand grab it and she screamed.

She began kicking furiously and succeeded in shaking the hand loose, but she lost her boot. She scrambled to her feet and crashed through the outdoor patio furniture, all covered for the winter, and ran for the barn out back. But her stocking foot slipped in the snow and she fell to her knees, cell phone in hand.

She started to cry as the Green Beret kicked out the laundry room door and stood there in the doorway, staring straight at her with his glowing night vision goggles. He thought he was so cool with his M4 with the attached laser site and grenade launcher. She knew what he was packing from her hundreds of hours playing the Red Glare game, and the one place he was now vulnerable. She jumped up and snapped his picture with Carla's phone camera, the flash blinding him in his overexposed goggles for a few seconds. Then she ran like hell toward the barn.

She rounded the back of the barn, opened the small side door and ran inside and opened the big double doors. Then she grabbed her saddle off the stake in the wall and ran to Punk's stall. She strapped the saddle on his back, her freezing hands fumbling with the buckles, trying to get it tight. She slipped her socked foot into the stirrup and hoisted herself up. Punk stamped his hooves and coughed. He didn't want to go out into the cold.

"Please, Punk. Please."

She kicked him again with the heel of her one boot, and Punk bolted out of the barn, knocking over the goon with the M4. It went off with a loud crack into the dark skies. She looked back and saw him slip onto his back on the ice while his partner rounded the house and raised his M4.

She slapped Punk's neck with the reins, and the horse jumped onto the adjoining trail.

Punk slipped on the snow and for a moment Jennifer thought he was going to fall on top of her. But he regained his balance and quickly galloped through the two feet of powder along the neighbor's wooden fence.

Suddenly the fence seemed to move and Jennifer heard a loud crash. A black Suburban crashed through the wooden rails onto the trail behind her.

"Oh, God!"

Jennifer kicked Punk as hard as she could, almost breaking the horse's skin with her boot. She screamed in frustration.

The Suburban, its high beams on, was only a yard or so away, its engine groaning loudly.

Punk picked up his pace with a new surge of momentum.

Jennifer looked back to see the Suburban fall behind momentarily. Then with a grunt and a spin of its wheels, it dug into the snow and zoomed up toward her with no intention of stopping.

Jennifer rode Punk along the narrow trail, the Suburban closing the gap as Punk started to tire, his powerful neck bulging with the strain. Just a little more, she thought, steering him toward the old McAllister place near the country club.

"You know where we're going, boy," she told him as he galloped. "We placed second in the Fall Hunter Pace, remember?"

They were riding along Guard Hill Road now, following a low stone wall, the Piney Woods Preserve on the other side, familiar territory to both her and Punk.

But the Suburban was moving up faster from behind.

Jennifer counted her paces. There was a break in the wall coming up. But it was hidden by the piled-up snow. Punk could leap through the gap and break through the snow, but he couldn't clear the wall if she misjudged the distance.

She kicked Punk and they picked up speed, the break coming up fast.

"Jump, Punk!"

She turned into the wall, gave Punk the right tug on the reins and closed her eyes. She felt the horse leap into the air and crash through the snow. The ice stung her face, but when she blinked her eyes open, they were into the trees of the preserve, Punk digging through the snow, his legs working furiously.

Behind her, the Suburban tried to stop but slid past the break in the wall on the trail. She heard a crash of metal. But she didn't dare look back. Punk galloped on into the woods.

CHAPTER THIRTY-ONE

1444 Hours
Air Force One

K oz was sitting on the gold sofa when Sachs emerged from the bathroom into the NCA commander's compartment, which was normally occupied by first-class passengers on a commercial 747. Her hair was wet and slicked back, and he had to admit she did more for the flightsuit that Captain Li had given her than Captain Li herself. Then he was ashamed for even thinking about his commander-in-chief in that way and pushed the thought out of his mind.

"Feeling better?" he asked her. He was sure he had heard her throw up in the bathroom. It was a natural reaction to her stress-inducing meeting with the National Command Authority, although he wasn't sure she'd admit to something seemingly unpresidential.

"Much." She sat down in the high-back leather chair at the desk and warily eyed the stack of executive orders he had brought her to sign, along with a steaming mug of hot tea. "Did you make this, Colonel? Or did Doctor Nordquist?"

It was almost funny, but he didn't dare crack a smile. "Captain Li did, ma'am."

"OK, I guess I have to trust her now—and you." Sachs took a sip, exhaled and looked around the compartment. "I just noticed there are no windows in here."

"Flash effects from nukes, ma'am. They can burn your eyes out. What windows we do have on the plane are made from the same stuff you'll find in your home microwave door."

"Of course," she said with a frown.

At first Koz thought she felt embarrassed by her technical ignorance. Or maybe she thought his microwave remark was as patronizing as Marshall's coffee order options. But then he decided she was simply sad.

She asked, "Where are we going?"

"We're following a pre-designated route to avoid enemy detection. We should be out of U.S. airspace shortly."

"No," she said. "I don't want us straying from U.S. airspace. We can't leave."

Koz muffled his real reaction, which was to lecture her on the realities of airspace and nuclear cloud bursts. But she would probably learn soon enough.

Sachs leaned forward and looked at the stack of Presidential Emergency Action Documents on her desk. "More proclamations?"

"You gotta sign them while you can," Koz said.

Sachs stared at the first one, an order freezing wages, prices and evictions. Then she signed with a flourish and said, "And I thought you were all Republicans," she quipped.

Koz cracked a smile. He was beginning to enjoy having her around, especially when everything else about the world right now felt so rotten.

"This one," he said, "is guaranteed to warm a progressive's heart."

He pushed another classified document across the desk for her to sign. It was a draft bill authorizing the IRS to collect money via a national sales tax of 30 percent.

"Whoah, Colonel. Sales taxes punish everybody. Even the federal response to the global pandemic never dared go to this extreme. Isn't the go-to solution supposed to be printing more money instead of taxing everybody?"

"Different scenario in play here, Madame President. We can't print our way out of this one. Not without making the dollar worthless and losing its reserve currency status. Then we're done, like Marshall said. For all we know, that's the win for them here. The nuclear threat is just for effect."

"With the risk that we go thermonuclear on them? I don't think so."

"Probably not. Besides, you needn't worry."

She looked up at him with a frown. "Why not?"

"This will all be over, one way or another, long before your order takes effect. Probably within the next 24 hours."

"Sure, Colonel. No worries." She signed the order, concluding that if money became worthless then it didn't matter how much you gave people to spend, because they still couldn't buy food with it. "And I'm not a progressive or conservative. I'm an American. Anything else?"

Koz slid a thick binder across the desk to her. "The latest National Strategic Target List," he explained. "It ranks more than forty thousand places and things in China, the Far East and elsewhere deemed worthy of destruction."

He watched as Sachs tentatively ran her finger down the list, pausing at a target and moving on. He could tell she couldn't do it, couldn't let her finger rest on any single item, knowing thousands of human beings would die if she did.

She said, "I guess I had forgotten that the United States has considered China its No. 1 enemy since the end of the Cold War."

"Until 9/11," Koz said. "General Marshall made his career at the Pentagon with his quadrennial reports stating that the war on terror in the Middle East had distracted America from containing the real threat in China. It wasn't until Trump and the coronavirus that originated in Wuhan that China came into play again publicly, mostly as a political football."

"But you think the threat from China has always been there, don't you?"

"No sugar-coating it, Madame President. China has been engaged in a secret war against the U.S. for years, aided and abetted by our feckless business and political leaders across both aisles. Hell, even Hollywood and the NBA. They sold us out, again and again. Pure greed."

She seemed surprised. "Then you think Trump was right?"

Koz was tempted to quip that even a broken clock is right twice a day. But he couldn't risk even a hint of bias on matters of national security, however politically inconvenient for himself.

"About China, yes. I take no sides with the facts, Madame President," he told her. "By the way, for every target you don't pick, you might as well put your finger on a map of the United States, because that's who will suffer instead."

"Thanks for the 411, Colonel."

"You wanted presidential authority," he reminded her and pushed a second operations manual at her, this one thicker than the first. "Now you have it."

"What's this?" Sachs asked.

"The Single Integrated Operational Plan," he explained. "The plan for destroying the places and things on the target list."

Sachs thumbed through the pages slowly. "This says that even after we and our enemies exhaust all our nuclear warheads and destroy the planet, America still has a secret reserve of nukes to fight on, post-Armageddon."

"That's right," said Koz. "The winner will be the one who can continue the battle and inflict still more damage. That winner will be the United States of America."

"But there will be nothing left to destroy! There won't be a homeland left for our bombers or subs to return to."

Koz said, "They could land or dock at foreign airstrips and ports. As you'll see, secret treaties with foreign allies would enable our government to survive as a political entity even if the United States itself were destroyed."

"It just wouldn't have any people!" Sachs said.

"Which is exactly what the Chinese want you to focus on, Madame President. They've gamed this all out. They know they can't beat us full out, at least not right now. But they're betting that you don't have the political will to win a nuclear war at any cost."

He intentionally made his final words practically sound like an accusation. That's when he saw it: a flicker in her eye, the shock of recognition that, yes, she actually might fold in the end after all. Rather than concern him, it encouraged him to know that she saw the stakes. And by knowing the stakes, when the moment came—as it surely would—she might actually rise to meet it.

All she said was, "Thinking about this all day must drive Marshall insane."

"You have to be a little insane to dream up these nightmares in the first place."

"So why do we do it?"

"It's an insane planet."

She picked up her mug of tea and curiously looked at the decal on the side, which depicted an F-22 fighter jet and the tag line: *Air Force: When it Absolutely, Positively Has to be Destroyed Overnight.*

"Something wrong?" Koz asked.

"It's just that nothing today is playing out like the likeliest scenario detailed in this report." She tapped her finger for emphasis on a graphic of the Taiwan Strait, the 112-mile strait of water between China and the island of Taiwan. "This says the Chinese would attack Taiwan before they ever risked attacking a U.S. target, let alone our seat of government. It also says with 99-percent probability that such an attack would take the form of a thousand land-based cruise and ballistic missiles in China blasting over the strait to knock out Taiwan's defense shields, followed by invasion before our fighter jets and carrier groups could arrive on the scene. Even then, China wouldn't strike the United States itself."

She was good, Koz thought. He tested her further. "What exactly are the Chinese supposed to be doing?"

"According to Brad Marshall?" She didn't even have to glance at the report. "First, they're supposed to be hitting us at Kadena Air Base in Okinawa, hoping to strike before our F-35 fighters get in the air and thus knock out our best staging area for combat patrols. Second, they're supposed to blind us in the theater of war by knocking out our overhead communication and imaging satellites. Third, if necessary, they might launch their new anti-ship ballistic missiles at our carrier groups plowing toward Taiwan. But they've done none of those things yet."

"No, they haven't, Madame President," he told her. "But General Zhang has proven to be irrational in the past, and it sure looks like the Chinese hit D.C. and accomplished an unimaginable regime change in the United States. A regime change that put you in charge, Madame President, and your actions or lack thereof can only stoke speculation."

"Meaning I'm a Chinese sleeper of some kind?" she asked him.

He knew the idea was ridiculous, but he had to push. She had enough doubters already in the ranks of the military, and she couldn't afford having her authority questioned. "It was you, after all, and not the Central Locator that found a way for you to get out of Washington before the blast, ma'am. That's a fact."

"I am not an agent of any foreign power, Colonel," she said firmly, her brown eyes on fire with rage. "How can I prove it to any of you?"

"This will help." He reached into his pocket and removed an authenticator card with the presidential seal on it. "This secret code card will establish your identity as president to military commanders if you're ever caught away from secure communications facilities." He paused, and then gave her his warmest smile. "I know you're not a plant. But you might have to prove it to others. That card will help."

"Thank you," she said and slipped the card inside her flight suit's outside pocket.

Koz wasn't satisfied. "Not a secure location."

Sachs started to unzip the top of her flight suit.

Koz tried to keep a straight face as he watched her tuck it into her bra. He wasn't aware of an authenticator card occupying that kind of space before, except maybe for the time former president Bill Clinton lost his one night.

She asked, "How's this?"

"Better," he nodded as Captain Li opened the door in time to see Sachs adjust her boobs.

Koz leaped to his feet in embarrassment, as if he had been caught in some sordid act. "Captain."

"Excuse me," said Li without batting an eyelash. The iron-rod discipline of her days at the U.S. Air Force Academy—before they did away with the "harsh" rite of Recognition—had taken over. "NORAD reports a massive wave of Chinese missiles heading our way."

"Trajectory?" Koz demanded.

Li was grim. "They're silo killers, sir."

CHAPTER THIRTY-TWO

1445 Hours
Northern Command

U se them or lose them?" President Sachs repeated, making a face on the split screen inside General Block's office perch overlooking the underground operations center at Northern Command

"That's what I'm saying, ma'am," Block told her and Generals Marshall and Carver.

But he was more concerned with the two big screens in the control room below. The left screen displayed TOT MISL 50 — total number of Chinese DF-5 ICBMs launched. The right screen displayed TTG -34.07.12 — time to go before detonation. Meanwhile, six other screens providing real-time data from the USAF Space Command's early warning radar sites at Clear AFS in Alaska and

Beale AFB in California projected their trajectory toward Minutemen III missile fields in Montana, Wyoming and Colorado.

"These Chinese DF-5s are silo-killers," Block repeated. "We either launch our M-III's or lose them, along with the ability to retaliate."

He could see Sachs flinch at the either-or scenario, and sure enough she said, "Two options are a dilemma, General Block. Three options at least give us a choice. What about our satellites? Do we have any visuals from space? Or even our forward-deployed fleet in the South China Sea?"

"Our satellites over China were blinded minutes before the DF-5s launched, and neither our air base at Kadena in Japan nor the Seventh Fleet has a visual confirmation."

"Then maybe they haven't launched, General Block. Maybe this is a phantom missile strike generated by the Red Glare cyberweapon. Isn't it convenient that we're denied visual verification at the same time our radars are registering incoming missiles? General Marshall?"

Marshall looked surprised. "You're probably half right, Madame President. The Chinese technically could have used Red Glare to blind our satellites, but in political and military terms it would make no sense for them to fake a missile launch and prompt a massive U.S. nuclear retaliation."

"Not for the Chinese," Sachs said. "But maybe for another party."

There she goes again, Block thought, refusing to accept the obvious for some shadowy conspiracy.

Sachs addressed Brad Marshall again, and said, "General Marshall, do you agree with General Block?"

Block could only hope the kid could make Sachs see straight. Or use his baby blues to hypnotize her or something. Anything.

"I have to, Madame President," Marshall told her. "Right now, we have the advantage of not only firepower but accuracy in striking Chinese military targets. We would spare most of the civilian Chinese population while degrading their military's ability to destroy ours."

"Even if that prompts them to strike back?

"Well, it looks like they already have, Madame President. And if they haven't, I don't see how they could strike back if we hit them now while we can."

Block could see Sachs try to keep a poker face, like she was thinking it through. But that was two votes of the NCA to her one, with Carver left to cast his ballot.

"General Carver," she finally said. "If the Chinese attack is for real, and if we do lose our land-based ICBMs, will our nuclear-armed bombers and submarines survive the attack?"

Block knew Carver had to nod a yes, which is what he did.

Then Carver said the only thing he could in his position: "The airborne and seaborne legs of our defense triad will indeed survive, Madame President, with enough firepower to destroy the world several times over and, per our war plan, preserve the continuity of government for the United States of America."

Block could see that was enough to satisfy Sachs and give her what she needed: a 2-2 split between the four of them. Worse, she clearly interpreted her vote as commander-in-chief to count as two in a tie.

She said, "So we can live without land-based ICBMs."

We can live without ICBMs? Block sensed that this failed Cabinet secretary was losing her grip on reality.

"You realize, of course," Marshall cut in, "that if you allow the enemy to attack yet again without retaliation, you'll only encourage further aggression against us."

Block watched her reaction on the screen. The woman looked positively constipated.

"General Marshall, you're the one who told Congress that great care and billions of dollars have been spent to construct American nuclear weapons systems that will survive a nuclear attack," Sachs replied testily. "The point was to give the civilian Commander-in-Chief—that's me, not you—the luxury of determining his or her response after the shape of the battle is clear."

Marshall said, "Except in this case you're letting the enemy shape it."

"No," she insisted, summing up. "We've got conflicting signals about the reality of this incoming attack. Northern Command says DF-5 silo killers are coming our way. But our satellites show nothing. The best course of action is to ride this out and determine our response after the shape of the battle is clear."

Ride this out? Block thought with almost unbearable frustration. *This has nothing to do with conflicting signals. She's incapable of pulling the trigger.*

"With all due respect, Madam President," Block said, knowing the inflection in his voice sounded anything but respectful, "the shape of this battle looks pretty clear on my screens, and that looks like one big mushroom cloud over Cheyenne Mountain in 24 minutes and 53 seconds."

"Then I suggest you prepare for impact," she said. "General Marshall, please send me a prioritized target list for those Mavericks you talked to me about earlier. Those bunker-busters we've got up in the air now that we can always recall. I think you called it the Tall option."

She had to put that little tweak in the nose at the end, thought Block. Couldn't leave well enough alone. But at least this was something.

"On its way," Marshall said and cut out.

Sachs moved on to Carver. "General Carver, American citizens have to prepare themselves for any eventuality. Issue a national attack warning. Move our subs into attack position. I want every plane from Kadena and the USS George Washington airborne. We'll reconvene five minutes before impact. Over."

Sachs disappeared from the screen, leaving Block on the video conference with Carver at Strategic Command. If anything, Carver was the one most at risk here, as Block always considered Cheyenne Mountain a far more formidable fortress than Carver's underground operations center beneath Offutt Air Force Base in Omaha.

Block said, "I say we go ahead and launch."

Carver frowned. "You can't be serious!"

"Come on," said Block. "What are we talking about here? A woman who can't make up her mind. I say we remove her from the chain of command."

Carver was adamant. "We can't do that, Block."

"Technically, the National Command Authorities are running the show now. That's us. She's only one vote out of four in the NCA."

Carver said, "She *is* our commander in chief."

"What the hell kind of commander in chief is this, Carver?"

"The only one we've got, understand? Look, she'll come around. It's Colonel Kozlowski and Captain Li who are advising her."

"The Polack and the Miss Saigon," Block said. "Sachs has got a goddamn rainbow coalition behind her. All she's missing is a Vulcan."

"Just prepare for impact," said a stone-faced Carver, obliging him with the split-fingered Vulcan "live long and prosper" salute from *Star Trek*. "I'll sound the National Attack Warning."

CHAPTER THIRTY-THREE

1450 Hours
Bedford Trails

Air raid sirens blared as Jennifer and her horse Punk rode beneath the frosty canopy of the Piney Woods Preserve. She feared she had only minutes to lose the Green Berets before they and every police unit in Westchester County converged on the area. She had to disappear, go somewhere nobody would ever consider, not even her mother.

There was Union Cemetery up ahead, or the Bedford Golf Club to her right. Either way, she'd have to emerge from the protection of the preserve to cross Clinton Road.

She dismounted Punk in the preserve and gave him a slap on the rump to make him move away from her. Then in one boot and one cold stocking

175

foot, she ran across the narrow, unplowed road. She clamored over a tall, green chain link fence on the other side and dropped along the 17th fairway of the Bedford Country Club. It dated back to 1892. Practically Neolithic-era, she thought, as she ran toward the majestic clubhouse beyond the 18th hole.

She skirted the clubhouse and went around back to the small, decrepit caddyshack, where Robbie had taken her to make out twice. Well, maybe one-and-a-half times. Nobody would expect to find her here, she decided, because it's the last place she expected herself to be right now.

She crunched through the snow to the freestanding mailbox in front of the caddy shack. She cracked open the icy latch to find dozens of score cards and pencils—and a key taped to the bottom. She pulled it out and looked back to make sure enough snow was falling to cover her tracks, but it would be a good half hour before that would happen. She realized she had no choice.

She locked the door behind her and shivered in the darkness. It was almost as cold inside the caddyshack as outside. She waited for her eyes to adjust in the dim light. First, she had to find out what was going on in the world. Then she had to decide whether she should use Carla's phone. She wanted to send her mom that picture of the Green Beret, but she didn't want to risk giving her location away to the goon and die.

She opened the broom closet and saw the words "R&J 4eVer" etched into a wall. Beneath the etching was an old AM/FM/CD boombox. She took out the boombox and put it on the floor, then wrapped herself with the dusty beach blanket she had stashed on the shelf weeks ago and sat down.

She said a quick prayer and hit the "on" switch. The boombox still worked. Batteries and everything. She turned up the volume and adjusted the dial.

"This is the National Warning Center," said the voice of God, or so it sounded. "Emergency. This is an attack warning. Repeat. This is an attack warning."

A bleeping sound started to repeat itself, then her mom's voice came on. Jennifer leaned closer to the box.

"This is President Sachs with a warning that another attack is imminent."

Jennifer gasped. "Oh, God."

"The threat appears aimed at U.S. military targets, not population centers. So there is little to gain in mass evacuations or hysteria. The best thing every American can do at this moment is to simply take cover in basements, schools, offices, churches, synagogues and mosques until the threat passes."

Jennifer looked around the sorry interior of the caddyshack. It had no basement but was about as good as anywhere else at the moment.

"Local police departments and National Guard units will be patrolling streets to enforce safety and use deadly force against those who would see this crisis as an opportunity to break the law."

What about those Green Berets chasing me? Jennifer wondered.

"Rest assured that the United States armed forces are standing by to unleash the full fury of their wrath upon those states that have financed, equipped or harbored those who have attacked us. Until then, fellow Americans, our prayers are with you and our children. Help them, and help your neighbors."

Jennifer pulled out Carla's phone. She knew the government could track her even when it was off, but only if they knew what phone she had. As soon as she placed a call, they'd know.

The EAS announcer came back on. "This was a message of the Emergency Alert System. This is not a test. Repeat. This is not a test."

That was enough to remind her that she could not be selfish in times like this. If there was anything that she could report to her mom that would be helpful, she had to do it, even if it gave her away.

She turned the phone on, got a dial tone and punched in her mom's number. "Mom, pick up," she breathed.

Even as she heard the ringing on the other end, she saw a flash of light outside and ran to the window. There in the distance was that black Suburban, high beams shooting out its crumbled front end. It was tracing a long path across the vast course, following the buried golf cart paths. It was still a ways off. But the path could only end at the clubhouse, she realized, and then here.

Phone to her ear, Jennifer paced nervously. Light from an outside lamppost streamed through the dirty window, through which she peered with each turn. The Suburban had disappeared from view, and she paused.

"Please identify," said a woman's voice in her ear, not her mother's.

Jennifer jumped in surprise. Her call had gone through. But to whom?

"Jennifer Sachs, is that you?" the woman asked.

Jennifer didn't know what to say. She was scared.

"My name is Captain Li, Jennifer," the woman said. "I'm putting you through to your mother now."

Jennifer heard a click and then her mother's voice. "Baby, where are you?" She sounded both relieved and frantic.

"I can't say yet, Mom. This line isn't secure."

"It's OK, I have people who can come and get you."

"Like the ones who killed Carla and almost killed me?"

"There was an audible gasp. "What?!""

Jennifer lost it then. She could feel her eyes tearing up. "They killed Carla, Mom. And if Aunt Dina wasn't out of town with her boyfriend, they would have killed her too. They're probably listening to me right now."

"Jennifer, please, tell me where you are."

Jennifer paused as she heard a distant wail of the national warning system sirens. "Like it matters now, Mom. We're all going to die. Just like Dad."

"Jennifer, I won't let that happen. Tell me where you are. I'll send help."

"No, I'll help you, Mom. I'm sending you a picture of the guy who tried to kill me." She found the photo on her phone and emailed it to her mother. "Just make sure whoever you send after me isn't him."

Suddenly two headlight beams pierced the window and the low hum of a distant vehicle grew louder. "Oh, God!"

Her mother's voice screamed through the phone. "Jennifer!"

Jennifer ducked and then peered through a corner of the window. The black Suburban with the crushed front end braked to a squeaky halt outside. The two Green Berets stepped out like something out of Red Glare.

"They found me!" she breathed into the phone and hung up.

CHAPTER THIRTY-FOUR

1501 Hours

Air Force One

Now it was Sachs who lost it, screaming into the phone, "Jennifer!" She sank to her knees and burst into tears, unable to hold back. It all came out, everything she had bottled up since the morning: her separation from Jennifer, the chopper crash, her lock-up in the infirmary and the strain of circumstances.

She felt Koz put a consoling arm around her shoulders and let him help her up before she pushed back and brushed her hair from her angry eyes. "Captain Li had better sure as hell traced that call, Colonel."

"I'm sure we'll be hearing from her any second with a location, ma'am."

On cue, the door slid open and Captain Li entered with her tablet displaying a map of suburban New York. "She called from somewhere inside the Bedford Country Club, Madame President."

Sachs could only wonder how Jennifer ended up there. "The photo." She opened her email. There was nothing but old messages that had stopped when the nuke had gone off that morning—a lifetime ago. "I didn't get it."

"We got it, ma'am," Li said. "We grabbed it from her outgoing email server. This is the man." Li tapped the display, and a blurred image of a Green Beret lunging toward the camera came into view.

"Oh, my God!" Sachs said, unable to mask her fear. "That monster is after my baby?"

"Yes, ma'am. We're trying facial recognition, but between the face paint and blurred picture, we haven't found anything yet. This guy is low-ranking."

"But he's one of Kyle's Green Berets who tried to kill me. How hard can it be to ID him?"

"He's doesn't the profile for anybody in Kyle's unit," said Captain Li, pausing. "I have to make something clear, Madame President. The U.S. military does not as a policy enlist or create monsters. But every now and then we do uncover some.

Sachs appreciated where Li was coming from, but would have none of it, not right now. "These are the same guys who tried to kill me." She turned to Koz. "These are Kyle's Green Berets, I know it. And you still haven't told me who he might have been taking orders from."

"I was going to tell you, but more pressing matters, specifically this imminent nuclear strike, got in the way," Koz began. "The short answer is everybody."

"Everybody?"

"I mean everybody, ma'am. It's not like Kyle was some cipher who had some doctored or classified record anybody was trying to hide. He's been everywhere in Iraq and Afghanistan and Pakistan and Iran, you name it. And he's crisscrossed with just about every senior officer in all branches of the armed forces. He even saved Marshall once when Marshall was a major and his bomber went down in Iraq during Desert Storm and the Republican Guards were closing in on him."

"That's something, Colonel."

"But it was Block who sent Kyle's team to find Marshall in the first place, ma'am, and Carver who got Navy SEAL support for extraction. Like I said, Kyle was the go-to guy for impossible missions."

"No wonder they all looked at me like I was crazy when I said Kyle was trying to kill me."

"They just figured you—or your Secret Service detail—confused his tough-guy tactics to save you with a threat on your life, and that's what may have inadvertently started a firefight aboard your chopper."

"So that's how the story is going down?" she said, angrier than ever. "How are they going to explain Jennifer?"

"They're not, ma'am, because we're going to get her first," Kozlowski said. "I have just the trustworthy team to reach her in less than 80 minutes. I would trust them with my life. Captain Li, please see if you can reach the RATS."

Li paused. "The blast, sir."

"If anyone survived it, they did," Koz said. "I want them moving the second after impact and any EMP."

"Yes, sir," she said and left Sachs alone with Koz.

Sachs put her hands over her face. "Oh, my baby, Jennifer. I couldn't even tell her that she saved my life. She's the reason I'm alive. If it wasn't for her, I would have been in Washington this morning when..."

Kozlowski handed her a handkerchief. She dabbed her eyes, embarrassed by her emotion.

"Thanks," she told him, and tried to hand back the handkerchief.

Koz refused. "Keep it. It's yours."

She then noticed the presidential seal in the pattern and managed a weak smile. "I never expected any of this when I woke up this morning."

"None of us did, Madame President."

Sachs shook her head. "Oh, I think somebody did, Colonel. And we're going to find out who that somebody is, for the sake of our families and our country."

"You can call me Koz, ma'am. Everybody else does."

Sachs took a breath, then looked at him differently. He had succeeded in breaking her emotional state, which she realized was not in a good place for the commander-in-chief. "So, Koz, where's your family?"

"Only a brother in Wyoming now. His backyard abuts a missile field. He knew the risks. Hell, we all did."

Sachs asked gently, "Nobody else?"

He shrugged and smiled. "Don't meet a lot of women up here."

"Captain Li sure is a fan."

Koz dropped the smile, not allowing a hint of ambiguity. "Strictly professional, ma'am."

Sachs felt strangely relieved. "I'm sure it is, Koz. And you can call me —," she said when suddenly the plane pitched and rolled, slamming her against the bulkhead and knocking her out.

CHAPTER THIRTY-FIVE

1501 Hours
Looking Glass

Marshall also felt the shockwave from his general's quarters aboard the Looking Glass plane. He had escaped there a few minutes earlier to collect his thoughts and run through his checklists away from the crew. Now an alarm was sounding and there was an expected knock on his door.

"General Marshall, sir!" It was Quinn's quivering voice.

Marshall said, "Enter."

Quinn walked in, EAM printout in hand. "We lost STRATCOM, sir. Our home base!"

"Then the day has finally come, Colonel," Marshall said calmly. "Launch authority transfers to us here aboard Looking Glass. Shut the door."

Quinn, not quite understanding, turned to close the door. When he again faced Marshall, there was an open bottle of Jack Daniels on the desk. Marshall poured two glasses and handed one to Quinn, who didn't look like much of a drinker.

"Courage, Colonel, before the storm," Marshall said and raised his glass in a toast and gulped it down.

Quinn took a sip and coughed. "Sir, we have to get to our posts."

"We are at our posts." Marshall set down his glass. "Remember when I asked you for your launch key and told you to shoot me next time?"

"Yes, sir."

"This is next time." In one fluid movement, Marshall drew out his M9 sidearm and shot Quinn between the eyes.

The officer crumpled to the floor. With the ease of a weightlifter, Marshall grabbed Quinn's body by the leg with one hand and dragged it into his open closet. Then, before he closed the door, he bent over and removed the launch key from Quinn's neck and put it around his own.

CHAPTER THIRTY-SIX

1502 Hours
Air Force One

Sachs was on the floor groaning when the emergency lights kicked on and Kozlowski rushed over. She thought she heard him say, "Are you OK, Madame President?" But she wasn't sure. Her ears were ringing.

"What was that?" she asked as she let him help her to her feet. She felt wobbly.

He told her, "Omaha, I think."

She heard more ringing, but it was her desk phone beeping. Captain Li came through on the speaker. "NORAD has confirmed another nuclear detonation in the continental United States. General Block at Northern Command is onscreen in the conference center."

She felt Koz reach over her shoulder to the button and say, "The president is on her way."

The ringing had faded for the most part by the time she entered the conference room. Block's sour face was already on the big screen when she sat at the end of the table. Koz stood by her side. This was going to be ugly.

Sachs asked, "How many hits did we take, General Block?"

"Two," Block growled. "They took out our Tier-One Defender anti-ballistic missile site in Alaska and," he paused, glaring at her, "and STRATCOM."

Sachs swallowed. "General Carver?"

"That's right, Madame President," Block said, holding his stare. "This country has lost yet another great leader today, this time because of your indecision."

Sachs felt herself shaking. She desperately wanted to hold her voice steady. "Unleashing our Minutemen III missiles wouldn't have saved Carver."

"No, but he would have died like a soldier in the line of fire and not like a sitting duck," Block shot back. "And with our puny excuse for what was supposed to be a full, four-tier Defender system taken out, we have no way of intercepting the next wave."

She exhaled and paused. "General Block, what happened to all those other missiles the early warning systems said were supposed to hit?"

Block grew quiet. "Ghosts, ma'am. They were ghosts."

Sachs blinked. "How can several independent warning systems project so many false radar images?"

"At this point, ma'am, we have to assume it's the work of Red Glare, like you suggested."

"But why would they do this, knowing we might have launched?"

Block said, "I believe they did this to prove they knew you didn't have the political will to act, ma'am, and to prove their cyber superiority. If they can do this, they own our defense networks."

Sachs was bewildered. "Maybe. But what's the point of destroying the Strategic Command in Omaha if all its planes and nukes were already in the air?"

"Hard to say," Block said. "Because Marshall can still launch our land-based ICBMs from Looking Glass."

Sachs started. "Pardon me?"

"The Post Attack Command Control System, ma'am," Block explained. "If nukes destroy STRATCOM or other command centers on the ground, Looking Glass can command American forces from the air and launch our ICBMs by remote control."

"Let me guess," Sachs said. "The man who designed this brilliant Post Attack Command Control System is Brad Marshall?"

Block paused. "Uh, yes."

CHAPTER THIRTY-SEVEN

1503 Hours
Looking Glass

Marshall had assumed his command post in the battle staff compartment and was reviewing his NSTL targets in China on his digital tablet when Major Thompson beeped him.

He ignored the interruption. That he could reprioritize targets with a simple drag and drop on a handheld touch-screen display was something he never would have imagined even five years ago. Harney and Wilson, meanwhile, were establishing the SIOP operations plan with 50 ground-based launch control centers that controlled more than 300 Minuteman III nuclear missiles.

Thompson beeped him again. He saved his screen and spoke into the comm. "You're patching me to our B-21s with the Mavericks, Major?"

His hope was that President Sachs would finally use the simplest strategy he had gift-wrapped for her: the decapitation of the Chinese high command with the Maverick bunker-busters, followed by the swift threat of nuclear annihilation to any successors.

"I've got AF1 on line," she said instead, her voice hard and edgy. "Colonel Kozlowski is asking for Colonel Quinn."

Marshall noted several of the battle staffers, not part of his team, exchange glances before they got back to their work. He was playing for two audiences now. "Put him through on speaker."

"Here he is, sir."

Marshall pressed the button. "Marshall here. Has the president assessed the damage yet from the Alaska and Omaha hits, Colonel Kozlowski?"

"She's reviewing them now, sir."

Marshall nodded. "Then why are we talking?"

"The president would like to speak with your second, sir. Colonel Quinn. The roster says he holds the second launch key."

"Quinn is busy," Marshall said. "So am I. We're trying to re-establish links with several launch control sites that lost contact with Strategic Command. Those boys are in the dark and might launch if we can't reach them."

"That is a grave situation, General Marshall, and I will report it to the president. Nevertheless, launch authority for ground missiles has been transferred to Looking Glass. We must ensure procedures—"

Marshall said, "The Chinese have nuked Washington and STRATCOM. Now you want to quote regulations to me?"

"Yes, sir."

Marshall said, "Listen to me, Colonel. We have a commander-in-chief who can't pull the trigger. I need you. America needs you. The people of China, the real Chinese, need you. Are you on board?"

"Of course, sir."

Marshall said, "Then quit clogging secure channels. I'll reconvene with the president at the attack conference in six minutes. Over."

Marshall disconnected Kozlowski and hit his comm. "You catch that, Major?"

Thompson' voice said, "Yes, sir."

"Clear skies," Marshall said. He looked at Harney and Wilson, who had already drawn their M18 sidearms with silencers and began firing, taking out half the battle staffers while the others scrambled, too stunned to figure out what was going on. Thompson got them on her way in and then sealed the compartment shut behind her, breathless.

Marshall, disturbed that a bullet ricochet had nicked his forearm with a red skid burn, hit the comm again. "Cockpit now," he said, and another communications tech upstairs put him through to Captain Delaney.

Delaney said, "General Marshall, sir."

Marshall knew he couldn't hide everything from the Looking Glass crew, but he could spin it just enough to give him the time he needed. He had trained them all at one time or another, but he couldn't include them all in his plans. He was counting on personal loyalty and the cloud of war to bridge whatever cognitive dissonance was going through their minds.

"I want you and Rogers to seal off the cockpit, Captain," Marshall said. "Launch control from Offutt has been transferred to Looking Glass, and we've had gunfire here in the battle staff compartment. You know the procedures. Take us down to 18,000 feet and extend the VLF antenna. We need to establish links with both our underground launch centers and our submarines. No line-of-sight communications, not even AF1 for the time being. We can't reveal our location to enemy aircraft. If we are engaged, prepare to deploy all countermeasures at my orders."

"Copy that," the pilot said. "Over."

Marshall stared at the only three officers still standing in the compartment—Thompson, Wilson and Harney. Only Thompson had broken a sweat.

"A bit early, sir?" she asked.

"Sachs is on to us," he said and removed the two keys around his neck.

CHAPTER THIRTY-EIGHT

1504 Hours
Air Force One

Koz was still processing his bizarre and disturbing exchange with Marshall when he walked up to Captain Li on the communications deck. "Marshall blew me off," he told her. "Something's wrong."

"Way wrong, sir," Li said. "I have something the president needs to see."

Koz had them meet in Sachs' suite, where Li showed the president satellite surveillance video over Washington, D.C., before the nuke attack. She zoomed in on a railyard not far from Union Station.

"According to the last communications between the Pentagon and White House, it seems the nuclear device was delivered by rail on a Metro subway train right beneath the Pentagon," Li explained. "So I crosschecked D.C. police dispatch records, what's left of their remote backups, and learned that a Metro security guard was found slain this morning at this railyard."

Sachs remembered seeing the story that morning in the *Post*. "That's where the Chinese must have hitched the nuke to the train."

"Now watch this," Li said and zoomed in until two Chevy Suburbans popped out of the pixels. "Those are military plates, ma'am. And they're assigned to this man."

The picture on the screen changed and an ugly, familiar face filled the screen.

Sachs said, "That's Colonel Kyle, the Green Beret."

"And you'll recognize this other man, too," said Li. "He's the one after your daughter."

Sure enough, the next picture that came up matched the one Jennifer had sent.

Sachs leaned closer to the image, fear and rage swirling inside her. "You're telling me that these men—our men—may actually have betrayed America and helped the Chinese perpetrate this attack on our capital?"

Li said, "We think it's more likely they and the ones they report to are in fact behind these attacks and not the Chinese."

"Proof, Captain," Sachs demanded. "We don't have a lot of time here."

Captain Li nodded. "You can thank your daughter Jennifer."

"What?"

"I found this on her USB flash drive from school." Li pulled up Jennifer's PowerPoint presentation for school. The top slide of the deck was Brad Marshall waving to reporters aboard an aircraft carrier. As the slides flashed, Sachs was embarrassed at Jennifer's obvious hero worship—or more—for Marshall.

Li said, "This is a Time magazine photo of Marshall after he escaped Iraqi capture during the first Persian Gulf War in 1991. Kyle led the team that rescued Marshall when his plane was shot down."

There was Colonel Kyle, an arm around a beaming Marshall.

Koz said, "So Marshall and Kyle have a history. I've been through this with the president. It's not enough."

Li said, "How about this?"

Next up came a recent picture of Marshall inspecting the Tier-One Defender ABM complex in Alaska, and then a haunting longshot of him crossing the tarmac at Offutt AFB. Both came from a Time Magazine "Man of the Year" cover story titled "An American Hero: Forgotten But Not Gone."

Sachs said, "I still don't get it. You'd expect Marshall to be at these places. They're all he has left."

"Had left," Li said. "Both have been blown to bits. Before they were, each was visited by Colonel Kyle and other men from Marshall's past for base parties. Swipe card records place them all in highly sensitive areas at both bases."

Koz said it out loud. "One stolen SS-20 nuke. Three warheads. Each planted at a strategic location to make it look like a Chinese attack and force us to respond."

Sachs sat back in her chair, everything sinking in. "But why?"

"His wife." Koz said what they were all thinking. "She died from the novel coronavirus, and Marshall blamed the Chinese for it. Along with every American politician and tech titan who sold out to them."

"Too easy, Colonel. I blamed airplane manufacturers for my husband's death. But I didn't try to take them out." She shook her head. "I can't believe Marshall could hate his country's politicians so much that he'd kill thousands of innocent Americans."

Li said, "The rest of your daughter's report argues the opposite, Madame President. That Marshall loves America and feels his warnings about an ascendant China and declining America have been ignored. His very public statements underscore his belief that if we—the United States—don't act aggressively now, we will lack the weapons and will to do so later. According to that logic, he's saving American lives."

"And clearly will stop at nothing," Koz said.

"Even if that were true, Colonel, how on earth could one single general and a small team be capable of pulling off an attack of this scale without outside help? It's impossible."

"Between loyal officers throughout the armed forces and private contractors on the outside, and God knows who else, you'd be shocked at the kind of invisible army a general like Marshall could amass over the decades," Koz told her. "Especially now with his new command."

"That was a demotion for him," Sachs said.

"Was it?" Koz asked. "Madame President, we have to warn General Block at Northern Command to strip Marshall of launch authority immediately, before Marshall does anything crazy."

"Stop," said Sachs suddenly, thinking out loud. "Would Marshall have had access to this plane?"

Koz turned pale. "We share the same maintenance crews as Looking Glass."

Sachs said, "I want you to sweep for explosives right now.

CHAPTER THIRTY-NINE

1509 Hours

Four minutes later they all stood in the cargo hold, looking at an open box of toner cartridges wired together with enough explosives to bring down Air Force One in seconds. The red blinking light on the attached phone showed it was armed.

Koz swore. "God in heaven."

Sachs and Li stood behind him as he studied it. The red light bathed his face.

"Looks like Marshall tore a page from the Yemen terrorist playbook," he said. "Pack high explosives into printer cartridges to avoid detection by scanners. Poetic, too, since toners are used for all our EAM printouts."

Sachs said, "Still think I made up the attack on my chopper?"

Koz shook his head and studied the bomb. "This is bad," he said. "The phone still has its battery. That means it's not a timer. It's a remote detonator. Probably synced to the VLF receiver. That's what our submarines use to receive launch orders."

"Meaning?"

"Meaning Marshall can basically blow us up from any point on the planet as soon as we try anything. Hell, he might have been listening to all our internal communications all along too."

Sachs asked, "Just how easy is it for Marshall to launch our missiles?"

"Once the eight-digit enabling code is dialed into the launch system, the procedure is simple. It's not like a sub where you need several other officers involved in the launch. The Looking Glass plane is essentially a remote-control unit."

"But don't you still need two officers turning their keys at once to launch?"

"Trust me," he said grimly. "Marshall's already taken care of that."

"Then we have to somehow override the Looking Glass controls so he can't launch."

"Same problem. Assuming we can pull it off, he'll figure it out and vaporize us."

"Wait," Sachs told him, and he could see the wheels turning. "I have an idea."

CHAPTER FORTY

1510 Hours
Air Force One

S achs entered the cockpit, a finger to her lips and whiteboard in front of her. The two pilots and navigator looked up in surprise, then gaped as they read the words she had written:

Turn off your headsets.
Don't say a word.
Enemy listening.

The men exchanged glances, then slowly removed their headsets and turned them off.

Sachs said, "There's a bomb on board and we need to get off this plane. Preferably after we've landed safely on the ground."

The navigator scrambled to check his charts. "We're over the North Dakota badlands, ma'am. No airstrips or predesignated alternative bases in the vicinity, and Minot and Grand Forks are too far away."

"Improvise," Sachs said. "Find a stretch of highway if you have to. But make sure it's near a truck stop or some place with food and facilities. If we land in one piece, we'll need to set up a new command post."

As she left the cockpit, already she could feel the plane making a sharp descent. She rejoined Koz in the battle staff compartment, where he was poring over an operations manual while battle staffers worked furiously at their consoles.

Sachs leaned over Koz. "How are you doing?"

"It's tricky, but I should be able to override the Looking Glass launch procedures without Marshall catching on." Koz looked up at her. "I just don't understand why he'd do this. I do but I don't."

Sachs said, "Decapitation. By blowing up D.C., Marshall ensures we go to war with China — while we can still win it on our terms."

"Until you came along," said Koz, as he started reprogramming the overhead launch console.

Sachs said, "Well, clearly he made contingency plans. You said all Marshall has to do is dial in the eight-digit enabling code."

"Yep. Once you have the code, it's simple."

Sachs asked, "How simple?"

CHAPTER FORTY-ONE

1520 Hours
Looking Glass

Marshall waited until they had descended to 18,000 feet before he removed the key he wore around his neck and inserted it into one of two locks in the red safe next to his desk console in the battle staff compartment. He then removed the second key he had taken from Quinn and opened the second lock.

As soon as he opened the safe, the alarm went off, a clattering sound like a woodpecker. But there was no intelligence officer to stop him now. Nobody.

The launch procedure was so simple, really.

Let Deborah Sachs keep American bombers and subs at bay, he thought. He was going to launch the land-based ICBMs at China. At least he could be sure *they* would launch under attack. Then the war

213

would be underway. A war the United States would win.

Marshall waited a full minute before the clattering stopped. He then removed two more keys from inside the safe and tossed one to Thompson.

"The keys to the kingdom, Major Tom."

Marshall cracked open the code card with the eight-digit enabling code. He repeated it out loud:

"Tango, Seven, Bravo, Four..."

Thompson keyed it into the overhead launch console. "Tango, Seven, Bravo, Four," she repeated.

The corresponding beeps locked in the code.

Marshall read the final four digits. "Alpha, One, Delta, Nine."

"Alpha, One, Delta, Nine," echoed Thompson, and locked in the code.

Marshall then inserted his key into the overhead console. "On my count."

Thompson inserted the second key and nodded.

"Three..."

"Two..."

"One..."

"Turn."

Simultaneously they turned their keys.

CHAPTER FORTY-TWO

1520 Hours
Air Force One

It was a white-knuckle landing onto Interstate 29. Sachs felt Air Force One touch ground only to suddenly lift again and then set down. The pilots immediately threw the thrusters into reverse to try and stop it. But the plane wasn't slowing down and she couldn't see outside from the seat with the five-point harness that Captain Li had strapped her into.

"What's going on?" she asked, her voice shaking as her seat vibrated like an electric chair.

Captain Li put a finger to her earpiece. "There's a new overpass across the highway that wasn't on the maps. We had to jump it and now we're coming up too fast on another one."

This might be a real short landing, Sachs thought, but she knew that Marshall might launch missiles at any moment. She unbuckled her harness and stood up, her head immediately hitting an overhead bin she hadn't noticed before. Captain Li was on her feet and right there behind her.

"What are you doing, Madame President?"

Sachs rubbed her head. "Koz can't wait for us to stop to override Marshall's launch authority. He's got to do it now."

Li didn't try to stop her, but instead helped her move through the corridor to the battle staff compartment, where Koz and AF1 battle staffers were locked at their stations.

"Koz! We have to stop Marshall now!"

Koz was reading off his operations manual, punching in new authorization codes into the overhead consoles as the plane began to finally slow enough to make Sachs believe they were going to stop safely. "I think I've got it!" Koz shouted above the roar of the engines. "Off this plane, everybody! You too, Madame President."

She said, "I'm not leaving this plane without you, Koz."

"Yes, you are," he said and motioned to Captain Li and two officers, who grabbed her by the arms and began to drag her away.

CHAPTER FORTY-THREE

1520 Hours
Bedford Country Club

Jennifer backed away from the window as she watched the two Green Berets march toward the caddyshack. She ran back to the tiny kitchen that in the summer kept the caddies fed between golf rounds. She opened the pantry next to the refrigerator, which was unplugged. She pulled out the empty, removable stacks and shelves and hid them behind the fridge. Finally, she opened the back door a crack, to make it look like she had escaped. Then she hid herself in the bottom half of the pantry, ignoring the rat droppings. With a shiver she closed the door and held her breath in the dark.

She heard the front door rattle. A second later it was kicked open with a loud crash. She gasped and then clapped her hand over her mouth.

She could hear the soldiers check the sliders of the guns with a couple of loud clicks for effect, to signal they were coming after her, hoping she'd make a sound. She sat stone still.

One of the soldiers whispered, "Look."

They were at the back door.

Jennifer felt a draft as the back door was fully opened.

"Maybe," said a second voice. "Check it out."

Jennifer heard the front door open again, hoping against hope they were leaving, when she heard the floor creak inside the kitchen.

Oh, God, no.

Someone was standing directly on the opposite side of the pantry door. The door began to crack open. She was about to scream when the soldier's radio popped and the door closed.

She heard his gravelly voice say, "Copy that. We're out of here."

She listened to his footsteps walking out of the kitchen. Then she heard the front door open and shut.

A minute later, the heavy thuds of the Suburban's doors closed. The engine roared to life and then faded in the distance as it drove off.

CHAPTER FORTY-FOUR

1521 Hours
Looking Glass

ajor Tom turned her launch key a second time inside the battle staff compartment. Nothing. She looked at Marshall blankly.

"Turn!" Marshall repeated as he turned his own key.

Thompson tried one more time. Still nothing. "Sachs must have changed the enabling codes!"

Marshall stared at the two launch keys, both turned in their respective launch locks. "Goddamn that Koz!" he said, his nostrils flaring as he exhaled. "I think it's time we remove the final layer of federal bureaucracy."

Thompson nodded and moved to the consoles. She booted up yet another sabotage program. "Crash and Burn, sir?"

Marshall nodded. "Bye, bye, Miss American Pie."

Thompson pushed the delete button on her terminal.

CHAPTER FORTY-FIVE

1522 Hours
Ethel's Truck Stop Cafe

It was as bleak as the late afternoon could get in Drayton, North Dakota, population 913. Especially after two separate nuclear attacks on America. But Ethel's Truck Stop Café was open for business, as always.

The radio by the stove was playing "Everybody Wants to Rule the World" from the old rock group Tears for Fears. Which pretty much summed up the mood at the counter as Ethel with the blue hair poured another cup of coffee to rumpled Joe the truck driver when his cup and saucer started rattling.

Ethel stopped pouring and cocked her ear as she heard an ear-piercing noise outside. She had heard every kind of conceivable aircraft and missile in her lifetime around these parts, and knew it was a 747-

200 military converted jumbo jet even before she ran outside and saw it coming straight for the diner.

"Jeez, Louise!" she screamed. "Everybody take cover!"

She ran back inside and ducked behind the counter, staring at Rusty the waitress and poor old Joe, who wet his pants. The ground started shaking and plates were falling and crashing all over the floor. It sounded like a locomotive was passing straight through the diner.

And then, as suddenly as the roar began, it stopped, until there was only the sound of a rolling dish or two breaking.

Ethel cautiously poked her head above the counter and looked out the glass doors as the plane skirted onto the I-29 in three bumps and rolled to a stop about 400 yards from the café.

A moment later it exploded into a giant ball of fire, and Ethel ducked for cover again as the force smashed the windows, shards of glass raking the walls like bullets.

CHAPTER FORTY-SIX

1522 Hours
Northern Command

Now that STRATCOM was gone, General Block at Northern Command was suddenly having trouble communicating with America's three main Minuteman III forces: the 90th Missile Wing at F.E. Warren AFB in Wyoming, the 341st Missile Wing at Malmstrom AFB in Montana, and the 91st Missile Wing at Minot AFB in North Dakota. Together they controlled 450 ICBMs, and Block had to ensure transfer of launch authority from Carver to Marshall aboard Looking Glass.

He worried this was a Red Glare effect. A similar, inexplicable loss of communication between the control center at Warren AFB and 50 of its missiles had occurred months ago. Block had issued a statement at the time saying that the power failure was not malicious and that the Air Force never lost the ability to launch the missiles.

Which wasn't true.

"I hope you've got Marshall on for me," he said when his grim senior controller walked up.

"General, sir, we've lost Air Force One."

"Damn," Block said. "We've run out of presidents."

However much he disagreed with Sachs, he had admired her pluck.

"Well, there's no choice now. Tell Marshall he can authorize our B-21s to deliver the Maverick strike on the Chinese high command. Maybe the destruction of their host supercomputers will cut off Red Glare and release our missiles."

CHAPTER FORTY-SEVEN

1525 Hours
Bedford Country Club

Jennifer, her hand on the back of the pantry door, didn't move. She was afraid to come out. What if the Green Berets hadn't really left? What if one of them stayed behind? What if it was a trick? What if as soon as she opened the pantry door some guy with a gun put a bullet into her? She breathed slowly, listening for the slightest sound outside.

A minute passed.

Then five minutes, it seemed.

Finally, she could take it no more.

She burst out of the pantry and threw herself onto the kitchen floor, hands over her head, and screamed, "Don't shoot me!"

She heard herself crying and lifted her head, realizing there was nobody else in the caddyshack.

Slowly she got up and walked to the front window and looked outside. She could see the twin tracks of the Suburban leaving the club.

She ran to the back window and looked out too. Nobody there either.

She heard a creak overhead.

She looked up at the ceiling and had the terrible thought that maybe one of them was on the roof. Maybe they were waiting for her to pop her head out the front door and they would nail her then.

She looked around and saw a filthy broom in the corner of the main room. She picked it up and with a cringe of anxiety burst out the front door and thrust the broom outside.

But nothing happened. No shots. Just a dirty broom in the snow.

She was puzzled. Why did they leave?

She saw her blanket and radio in the corner and turned on the radio. The nerve-shattering signal of the Emergency Alert System blared.

The EAS announcer said, "This is the Emergency Alert System. The following is a message from the National Command Authority."

Mom, she thought with relief.

But it was a man who was speaking.

"This is General Brad Marshall," said the voice, which she suddenly recognized and felt a chill down her spine. "Minutes ago an enemy missile destroyed the plane carrying President Deborah Sachs."

Jennifer's knees buckled. She dropped to the floor.

"This further act of aggression will not go unanswered," Marshall announced. "I have ordered the United States Armed Forces to respond with their full fury and might."

Jennifer turned off the radio. She sat on the floor and let loose with tears and then wailed.

She didn't care who heard her now.

CHAPTER FORTY-EIGHT

1525 Hours
Ethel's Truck Stop Cafe

Sachs and Captain Li were running toward the diner when the plane exploded with a thunderous KABOOM. Sachs tried not to look back and be turned to ash, but she was worried about Koz, so she began to turn her head over her shoulder as she ran.

"No!" came a shout from behind.

Koz was flying toward her, tackling her like a shield as the force from the plane blew them off their feet and she felt herself hurl through the air over a snowbank. He intentionally landed on top of her, smothering her into the snow.

She couldn't breathe and struggled for more than a minute until he got off.

Koz asked, "Still in one piece?"

She gasped for breath and brushed the snow off. "You trying to kill me?" she asked when a second thunderous explosion sent a chunk of the fuselage flying over their heads.

Once again Koz face-planted her into the snow.

"Stop it!" she ordered when he let her come up again for air.

"You can court-martial me later," he told her as they stood up to survey the damage.

What was left of the Nightwatch plane—Air Force One—burned in smoldering ruins. Engine parts were strewn across the interstate. A broken wing stuck upright out of the frozen ground, glinting in the weak late afternoon sun.

Sachs said, "We need to contact Block at Northern Command and rescind Marshall's launch authority."

Koz pointed to his right, and Sachs saw it: Ethel's Truck Stop Café. "With Air Force One gone, Block is going to assume you're dead. How are you going to prove your identity?"

"With this," she said, and began to unzip her flightsuit.

She watched Koz raise an eyebrow and then smile when she flashed the presidential authenticator card he had given her.

CHAPTER FORTY-NINE

1548 Hours
Looking Glass

M arshall stood with his junior officers Harney and Wilson, staring blankly at the radar screens inside the battle staff compartment: The D-10s were in position, but the first-strike B-21s carrying the bunker-busting Mavericks were turning back.

"What the hell?" he said.

Thompson turned from her console, bad news written all over her face. "Bombers turning back, sir."

"I can see that," Marshall said. "Put me through to them right now."

She paused, putting a finger to her ear. "Northern Command is calling."

He nodded, and she put General Block through on speaker.

"Our bombers are retreating, Block," Marshall said. "Zhang already surrender?"

"Sachs is alive," Block said. "Just got the call."

Marshall didn't believe it. "You authenticate her?"

"Yep, and voice prints match too," Block said. "Listen, son. You're busted. The president wants to ground Looking Glass, pronto. You are to land at Grand Forks AFB, where a reception team will be waiting for you to turn yourself in. You'll be tried in a military court and executed for your treason."

Marshall blinked in disbelief. "I don't know what kind of horseshit Sachs is feeding you, Block. But pulling back our bombers now is going to cost us. Big time."

Block didn't like backtalk any more than Marshall. "You heard me, Marshall. Your pilots have been instructed to land Looking Glass immediately. And in case you have any trouble understanding, we've got a couple of F-22s on the way to escort you. Over."

Block disappeared from view, and Marshall was aware that his own, unreadable poker face was still plain to see for Thompson and the others. So he kept it that way on the outside. It wasn't hard. Because he knew exactly what to do next.

CHAPTER FIFTY

1625 Hours
Ethel's Truck Stop Cafe

Sachs watched pepper-haired Ethel pour her a cup of coffee while the TV blared the downing of Air Force One and her death. It was freezing with the shattered windows, and a dozen AF1 crew were taping plastic sheets from the surplus store in back to keep out the cold. Koz, meanwhile, was still on the pay phone talking to Block, having been unable to connect his phone with its satellite in space. They were trying to set up a call with General Zhang for her, to confirm he knew the U.S. was standing down and requesting the same.

Ethel asked her, "You really the president?"

Sachs said, "So they say."

"You spoiled everything, you know. Women have been running the country just fine for two hundred years, only our men didn't know it." Then she winked and walked off with her pot of coffee to serve the rest of the AF1 crew as if they had been her regulars for years. All 48 had been accounted for, thank God.

Koz walked over with a grim face. "Looking Glass landed at Grand Forks, but Marshall and three crew were missing."

Sachs stared at him. "How can they be missing?"

"They must have bailed in flight."

"From a 747? Is that even possible?"

"Not at 35,000 feet and 500 knots," Koz said. "But the pilots report that Marshall had ordered them down to 18,000 and 150 knots. That altitude and speed are about what the top extreme skydivers use, and Marshall and his threesome are trained paratroopers. Four sky suits are missing, and there are bodies on the cargo deck. Looks like they shot their way out the rear transport hatch."

"But where did they go? What does he hope to accomplish?"

Koz shrugged. "I have no idea. Looking Glass by definition circles the Midwest in a nuke attack, to be close to the missile fields. But the only active missile fields here in North Dakota are a couple of hundred miles away at Minot. There's nothing in this immediate area except abandoned missile silos.

Maybe he's going to hide out in one and keep us hunting for him for as many days as possible."

"He's right, you know," Ethel said, jumping right into the conversation. "We used to have a full missile wing here associated with Grand Forks AFB, until they closed it down, moved almost everything to Minot. That cost us a lot of jobs."

"Almost everything?" Sachs glanced at Koz.

Koz explained, "They still keep a few weapons storage areas around here that hold nuclear contingency weapons. And there's the old Safeguard complex in Nekoma, but that's been abandoned even longer than the silos."

"You sure about that?" Ethel asked him. "I've served more than a few strangers in recent—"

The cups and saucers on the counter started shaking again. The whole diner started to shake.

"Lordy, here we go again," Ethel said.

But Sachs knew there wasn't another Air Force One about to make an emergency landing outside. Out of the corner of her eye she caught a flame trail on the horizon.

Koz and Captain Li beat her outside to have a look.

She caught up and stopped cold at the sight of a 60-foot Minuteman III ICBM missile lift off into the sky at like a space shuttle launch. The ground quaked from rocket's thrust.

"Oh, no," Sachs said. "Marshall."

"Beijing's about 6,500 miles away," Koz told her, doing some quick math. "And that rocket is going 15,000 miles per hour."

"Which means we have 25 minutes until impact," she answered when another Minuteman blasted off.

And another.

And still another.

Sachs counted ten flame trails lifting off from the fields in a ring of fire that turned the early evening twilight into day.

CHAPTER FIFTY-ONE

1600 Hours
Bailey Family Farm
Launch Control Center

In the hour before the Minutemen launched, Marshall's dome-shaped parachute blossomed against the setting sun. Marshall let the cold wind blow him across the desolate winter fields toward the lonely clapboard farmhouse below.

He looked over at Thompson, Harney and Wilson, all doing fine on the descent. His jellyfish chute favored by U.S. paratroopers had been packed and ready aboard Looking Glass.

Special cuts in the fabric gave his chute more speed and greater steering capabilities, enabling him to avoid the grain silo on his right and turn into the wind to minimize horizontal speed as he landed.

He hit and rolled, then quickly detached from his chute. Then, with the others close behind, he pulled out his M9 and headed for the farmhouse.

The MP in a parka on the front porch looked surprised to see visitors and whipped out an older M-16. He was talking to somebody through an earpiece but froze when none other than General Brad Marshall walked up the steps. He relaxed and lowered his gun to salute.

"General Marshall," he said with relief when Harney leveled his own M4 and spat out a round. *Blam! Blam! Blam!* And the MP was blown through the front door.

Sixty feet beneath the farmhouse in the launch control center, red warning lights flashed on the consoles like the Fourth of July. The two launch officers in blue uniforms sat tight in their aircraft-style seats, trapped by their shoulder belts designed to keep them from being thrown by the shockwaves if they ever launched ICBMs.

The missileers were dead men as soon as Marshall came through the vault door. Wilson and

Harney shot them in the head. Thompson followed up by relieving them of their launch keys.

One of the launch officers was still alive, barely, and Marshall glared at Harney. Too many video games for these younger officers. They shot at faces to save bullets. But the pros always shot twice to confirm a kill. Worse, single shots to the head only dehumanized the enemy. And these launch officers were anything but. They were American patriots, and he needed at least one of them alive.

The launch officer groaned. "General Marshall?"

"It's OK, son," Marshall said, leaning closer. "We'll get you some help. Don't worry." Then he popped the kid in the chest with a second bullet from his M9 pistol. The launch officer slumped in his chair, blood draining out of him. Marshall straightened and said, "Major Tom, how long will it take you to retarget?"

She looked at her console. "Thirty-six minutes using the Command Data Buffer system."

"You have ten," Marshall told her. "Harney and Wilson, you'll need to strip some equipment here. I saw an Explorer parked outside. See if the MP upstairs has the keys in his pockets."

As they left, Marshall hovered impatiently as Thompson calculated the retargeting information.

"You're taking too long, Major Tom."

"More than two hundred attack options have been programmed into this computer, sir," she replied. "We just need to dial up the right war scenario. Those missiles that are supposed to go, go. Those that aren't, don't."

"You don't get it. I want them all going."

"Oh, that won't even take a minute—if you can live with collateral strikes."

"As long as the Chinese can't, Major, I can."

Marshall pushed the launch officer he had killed off his seat and strapped himself in. Thompson did likewise in the other chair and then made the final adjustments.

"Missiles are retargeted," she announced.

Marshall gave the order, "Insert launch keys."

Thompson inserted her launch key into her console at the same time he did.

"On my mark," he told her. "Three... two... one... turn."

They turned their keys simultaneously.

The shaking began, and Marshall tightened his belt with satisfaction. Missiles on screen filled the silo cameras with their exhaust flames.

Finally, things were going according to plan.

CHAPTER FIFTY-TWO

1625 Hours
Bedford Country Club

Jennifer decided that she'd had enough of herself crying over her mother and the end of the world. If this was the end of all things, she didn't want to go out like a scared rat in a crap shack. She would face the future full-on, even if it was a mushroom cloud.

She rose to her feet with the old beach blanket around her shoulders for warmth. The floorboards creaked as she walked to the front door. She paused at the door and took a deep breath. She wrapped herself tighter in the blanket with one hand and flung open the door with the other and shrieked.

Standing inches from her face was one of the Green Berets, so close they shared each other's frosty breath. There was alcohol on his. She then saw the open bottle in his hand.

"We knew you were here and were just waiting for you to come out," he told her, pushing her back inside and slamming the door shut. "But now that your mom is dead, I thought you could use some comfort." His lips twisted into an ironic smile. "You see, I'm from the government and I'm here to help you."

Jennifer was terrified. "Where's the other guy?"

"Ran home to mommy and the kids, seeing as this is the end." There was a wild look in his eyes. He believed it, and this terrified Jennifer even more. "It's a terrible thing when discipline in the ranks breaks down in a crisis. But I'm getting one last hurrah before we pop."

She took a swing at his face but he caught her hand and twisted it back until she cried out in pain. Then he pulled her head back by her hair and started dragging her kicking and screaming across the floor.

"Stop!" she screamed. "You're hurting me!"

He turned her over and thrust the neck of the bottle into her mouth painfully so that she choked as the fiery liquid poured down her throat. He laughed again, his eyes on fire as she struggled to breathe, feeling like she was drowning.

.

CHAPTER FIFTY-THREE

1625 Hours
Ethel's Truck Stop Cafe

Sachs stared at the ten missiles as they arched into the twilight. Disbelief dissolved into despair as she recognized the world as she knew it was ending. A black hole seemed to open up under her feet and suck the soul out of her.

"God, no," she breathed.

Koz, standing next to her, sounded flat and distant. "Minutemen out of the Nekoma missile field. It was supposed to be inactive."

Sachs simply could not believe what she was seeing. "They're going to China, aren't they?"

"Can't tell you until they explode," Koz said, looking grief-stricken. "But at fifteen thousand miles per hour, they can reach their targets in less than 30 minutes."

She said, "We have to destroy them."

The look on Koz's face didn't inspire hope. "Only way to abort is from the launch control center. We could try our sea-based AEGIS ABM systems with the Seventh Fleet, but they can't take out all 10 Minutemen. Our best bet would have been the Tier 1 Defender complex in Alaska."

Sachs grew icy calm. "What about this abandoned Safeguard complex nearby that you talked about? What was its purpose?"

"It was the original Defender system," Koz said. "Safeguard was designed to defend Minutemen silos around here from a Soviet or Chinese counterforce attack during the 1960s."

"By 'counterforce' you mean nukes like the ones the Chinese are about to launch in answer to the Minutemen that Marshall just fired?"

"That's right," Koz said. "The Safeguard missiles would hit the incoming Soviet or Chinese nukes, giving us the all clear to launch a second wave of missiles."

"Punishing them even harder."

"Nice option for us to have now, right?" Koz said. "But it was operational for only four months before they shut it down. Been abandoned for decades."

Sachs said, "You mean like those Minuteman silos we just saw shoot off?"

Koz stared at her like she was either crazy or crazy brilliant. "You think Marshall built his new Defender system on top of the old Safeguard?"

Sachs nodded. "Marshall isn't a lunatic. He wouldn't let those missiles off unless he was confident he could shoot down any DF-5s the Chinese launch back at us."

Koz's face fell. "It's at least 40 minutes to Nekoma. We'll never make it in time on these roads."

"Stop telling me what we can't do!" Sachs lost it there, punching him squarely in the chest. "You dumb bastards!" she screamed, pummeling him again and again with her fists. "You're going to blow up the world with your pissing contests."

Koz took the blows stoically, waiting for her to stop.

Sachs calmed down, the missile roar faded, and there was only a ghostly cold wind until she heard the unmistakable snap of gum and turned to see Ethel standing behind them.

Ethel said, "I know how you can get there in 20 minutes."

Sachs stared at her, daring her. "Tell me."

"Same way me and Rusty got here this morning."

.

CHAPTER FIFTY-FOUR

1635 Hours
Pembina Trail

The icy Pembina Trail wound through several ghost towns and rivers toward Nekoma's infamous Safeguard complex. The snow-covered prairies glittered under the sparkling night skies. Sachs wrapped her hands around Koz's waist as he leaned forward and kicked up the speed of Ethel's four-stroke Yamaha snowmobile. She looked back at Captain Li, further behind on the trail, trying to keep up in Rusty the waitress's two-stroke Thundercat.

"This sucker can go 110 mph and stay there all day long," Ethel had promised them back at the truck stop diner, and Koz was determined to max the 145 horsepower to reach the Safeguard complex inside of 20 minutes.

Sachs felt herself slipping and tightened her grip on Koz, but her hands were too numb to feel. Her face was a frozen mask in the wind. But she could feel her heart pounding out of her chest. The stillness before the coming nuclear storm was ghostly, and she and Koz were just vapors in the early night.

"The land that time forgot," Koz told her, and she was surprised how clearly she could hear him. "That's one of the reasons the Safeguard complex closed down. Not much around to support it in terms of people or any kind of economy this far out from the Grand Forks base, which itself is nowhere to the rest of the world. You won't believe it when you see it."

They went over a snowdrift and there was the bleak Safeguard complex, a 435-acre missile field, dominated by a mysterious pyramid structure 80 feet tall and a dozen Stonehenge-like monoliths. It looked positively evil, like the technological ruins of some Cold War Giza plateau.

She said, "What are those spooky towers?"

"Intake and exhaust stacks for the missile site's power plant," Koz said.

"And that giant pyramid thing with the weird circles on each side?"

"The radar building," Koz said. "The control center for the whole Safeguard system. It housed the computers and radar that could track incoming ICBM warheads and hit back with 30 long-range Spartans."

She said, "But it looks so sinister."

"It was the era," he said. "But, yeah, it's got a Death Star vibe."

The drove straight through the open gate in the chainlink fence, where two slain U.S. Army guards lay in the blood-stained snow, beneath a sign that said: *Stanley R. Mickelsen Safeguard Complex.*

"Vibe?" Sachs repeated. "The era is now, Koz, and Marshall is Darth Vader."

"Then he's probably inside the pyramid," Koz said and followed the SUV tracks in the snow to the tunnel entrance to the pyramid, where they climbed off the snowmobile and Koz pulled out his M9.

An SUV sat just outside the tunnel.

"It's from the launch control center Marshall hit," he said, inspecting the vehicle as Captain Li pulled up on her Thundercat.

Li had the schematics ready on her phone's display. "The radio room is inside the turret at the top of the pyramid. Marshall and his radio gal Thompson are most likely up there. The other two officers missing from Looking Glass, Harney and Wilson, are his muscle. We'll probably encounter them before we ever get near Marshall. By the way, the first two levels inside are probably flooded from a few years back when contaminated PCB chemicals were cleaned out. So we'll have to wade through."

Sachs hid her alarm at this matter-of-fact description of the hell she was about to enter. Swimming through toxic waste wasn't exactly at the top of her life bucket list. But in this moment, such concerns weren't even worth bringing up.

"Let's go," she said when Koz blocked her.

"You're going to need this," he said, handing her a loaded M18 pistol, just like his own and Captain Li's. "The safety is off. So know that when you point and shoot, a bullet is going to go flying out. Squeeze slowly, be ready for some kickback."

Sachs nodded as she felt the gun. It looked like one of Jennifer's toys, but there was just enough heft in it to betray its lethality.

They started through the tunnel into the subterranean levels of the pyramid. At first it was just ice on the ground they had to watch out for. Then the hardness loosened to liquid the further they got inside, rising from ankle-deep to knee-deep to waist-deep in the arena-sized cavern.

Sachs could barely make out oil storage tanks and industrial waste sumps in the dark of the basement level. And she had to take it on faith from the dim glow of Captain Li's screen that they were passing the oil pumping room and transmitter cooling area of the pyramid.

Sachs said nothing and slogged through the foul-smelling chemical swamp until she was almost neck-deep. Never in her worst nightmares had she ever imagined herself in a place like this. They made it to a narrow concrete stairway and, dripping industrial ooze behind them, slowly climbed one crumbling step at a time.

The thin coat of oil weighed her down like a suit of heavy armor. As she tried to wipe it off, she slipped and almost fell off the steps. Were it not for Koz's hand, she would have surely plunked into the inky cesspool below, never to come up again.

"That was close," he whispered.

"You're telling me," she breathed as they finally reached the second level of the pyramid—the empty and thankfully dry shell of the abandoned command and control areas.

No Marshall.

Koz pointed up into the turret above.

Oh, God, she thought, *not another level.* Each one seemed more sinister than the last.

The third level occupied the lower portion of the turret, and it, too, was an empty tomb. This seemed to bother Koz and Li.

"See," Koz pointed out to Li. "The Duplexer area is gutted of its microwave devices associated with the radar receivers. Marshall would have had to have replaced them to make this active again."

All that remained was the fourth floor in the upper portion of the pyramid's turret. But because all 16 sets of stairways and elevators were removed when the building was salvaged, there was no way to reach it.

They skirted along the concrete wall until they reached a new steel ladder running up the wall to the fourth level. Koz pointed up to the dim square of light way up at the top, where a shadow flickered past the light.

Marshall was up there.

Koz started climbing the ladder with one hand while his other held up the M9. Sachs started right after him, but Li held her back until Koz was almost out of sight above her. Then Li gave her the go ahead, and Sachs put her boot on the ladder and pulled herself up.

As she did, one of Marshall's men emerged from the shadows like a phantom, moving quickly toward the base of the ladder. She heard a cry and looked down in time to see Captain Li fall away, shot in the back, dead.

Glowing eyes—night vision goggles—looked up at her from below and a red target dot began to move up her body. She struggled to find the gun on her hip but couldn't get it out of the holster. A shot rang out and the green eyes exploded in front of her and the phantom sank back into the dark.

She looked up at Koz, hanging on with one hand, the M9 in his other hand. "Look out!" he shouted as he aimed his gun at her.

Sachs flung herself to the side of the ladder, hanging on for her life while Koz pumped several bullets straight down the ladder at a second phantom. Sachs heard a groan and saw a fleeting shadow before she heard a loud *kerplunk* three levels below.

She tried to swing her feet back onto the ladder, but a couple of bullets pinged off the rungs. She looked up. Above Koz, a woman in uniform was leaning over the open ceiling door, firing down at them. Koz fired back one-handed, and the woman cried out and staggered back out of view.

CHAPTER FIFTY-FIVE

1640 Hours
Safeguard Complex

Inside the 30-foot-tall turret of the pyramid, Marshall was booting up his Defender air traffic controller post when he heard the gunfire erupting below. The only reason he had kept the floor's door open for the ladder was for Harney and Wilson, but he would close it if he had to and they would have to fry.

"See what's going on downstairs with Harney and Wilson, Major," he ordered Thompson, who was setting up the landline communications system and running a line on the floor.

"Yes, sir," she said.

Everything in the turret had been hardened to withstand nuclear impact: The walls, ceiling and floor were lined with an 11-gauge steel liner plate.

Mounted on the floor were open frame racks for circuit boards and built into each of the four slanted walls was a gigantic, 20-foot disc—the complex's phased-array antenna. Suspended overhead was a shock-isolated platform for Cold War support equipment long gone. The only thing it supported now were the servers that hosted the Red Glare cyberweapon program.

He turned his attention back to his radar screens and to opening a clear line of communications with his Defenders on the secret frequency. He was using one of Raytheon's newer STARS, or Standard Terminal Automation Replacement System equipment, to get a clear picture of aircraft operations over the Pacific airpace.

The digitized blips on the screen represented his ten top-secret Defender 747s armed with laser canons. They were the Tier 3 component of his Defender system, based on America's Airborne Laser Test Bed program. Each Defender plane could direct energy to attack multiple targets at the speed of light, at a range of hundreds of kilometers, and at a lower cost per intercept than missiles.

He could only imagine the look on General Zhang's face any minute now when he launched his DF-5s in response to the incoming American Minutemen nukes. The onboard sensors of the U.S.

Defenders would detect the boosting Chinese missiles and track them with a low-energy laser. A second low-energy laser would measure and compensate for atmospheric disturbance. Finally, the Defender would fire its megawatt-class high-energy laser, heating the boosting DF-5 to critical structural failure.

And General Zhang would see the futility of his response even before the incoming Minutemen killed him.

Marshall spoke into his headset, "All Defenders report."

Defender One reported, "All clear."

"All clear," reported Defender Two.

Every Defender, save Defender Six, was almost in range to shoot down any outgoing ICBMs from China that General Zhang might launch before he lost them to incoming Minutemen. Zhang's window was closing fast to make a decision, and so was Marshall's to make sure the Defenders could take out any Chinese missiles.

"Defender Six, climb to 38,000 feet," Marshall ordered.

Marshall knew from personal experience as a fighter pilot that the hardest part of mission flying was reading the clouds. Aiming a laser canon in flight was infinitely harder. Volatile temperature and barometric pressure might bend the beam just enough to miss an outgoing missile or jiggle the plane enough to blow the shot.

Defender Six updated its position. "Barometric pressure stabilizing."

Marshall said, "Maintain course, Defender Six."

Marshall had trained these pilots well, and the beauty was that nobody in the current situation knew about them. Not General Zhang in China nor General Block at Northern Command. Only President Rhinehart and General Carver at STRATCOM, who allowed Marshall's program to proceed behind Congress's back. Now they were both dead.

Best of all, at this time of year in January, Beijing was cold but dry, with an average of fewer than two days of rain.

In short, its clear skies were perfect for lasers.

Marshall heard Thompson cry out and turned to see her stagger back from the open door in the floor and collapse. He pulled out his M18 and walked over. She was spitting up blood, suffering, eyes pleading for help.

Marshall gazed down at her for a moment. She reached up her hand, and he took it in his left even as he lowered his right hand holding his M18.

"Mission accomplished, Major Tom." There was pride in his voice, but no pleasure as he put her out of her misery with a bullet to the head. "You are honorably discharged."

The light went out of her eyes instantly, and her head rolled to the side.

Marshall moved to the open door in the floor and peered over the edge, cautiously. He saw none other than Colonel Joe Kozlowski coming up the ladder, with what appeared to be Deborah Sachs some way behind him. Kozlowski was pointing a gun up at him, and Marshall moved back as a bullet whizzed by his ear.

Marshall stuck his hand holding his gun over the edge and sprayed several bullets straight down until Kozlowski stopped firing.

.

CHAPTER FIFTY-SIX

1645 Hours

Sachs heard the gunshots and called out Koz's name. But instead of an answer she saw him suddenly lose his grip and fall toward her. She grasped the next rung of the steel ladder with one hand and swung out of the way. She watched in horror as Koz's body hit the concrete floor at the base of the ladder far below.

She screamed. "Koz!"

Above her, Marshall's face lingered in the opening, gun in hand, but then withdrew from sight.

She froze on the ladder. She desperately wanted to crawl down to Koz and run away from that monster Marshall above her. But run to what? A world that Marshall destroyed? There was no turning back, she realized. This was either kill or be killed, and she had to keep going. Jennifer and at least a billion American and Chinese lives were counting on her.

Sachs willed herself up the ladder, one rung at a time, hand over hand, boot over boot, until she reached the opening. She wanted to stick her gun through and start shooting, but she needed both hands to pull herself up and over onto the steel floor of the top-level turret.

The moment she made it over, she instantly sprang to her feet and whipped out her gun, breathing hard. She looked around turret cautiously, but nobody was there as far as her eyes could see. Nobody but the dead radio operator sprawled against the wall, an M9 on the floor beside her.

Sachs kicked the pistol over the edge of the floor door and scanned the austere, two-story-tall turret. Dominating the chamber were something like huge loudspeakers in each of the four slanted walls. The effect was like being inside the bell tower of some monstrous cathedral from the Dark Ages—the Church of the Apocalypse. And the altar seemed to be a console with communications and radar instruments.

She noted the large, square radar screen with a Raytheon logo on the bezel and a large brown keyboard with four different sets of keypads grouped on it, along with the biggest computer mouse—made of metal—that she'd ever seen.

It was some kind of air traffic controller's radar screen. There were ten arrow-like icons, and they were moving toward China.

The Defenders aren't anti-ballistic missiles. They're airplanes.

And they were poised off China to shoot down any Chinese missiles.

There was a step behind her. She turned and raised her M18 as Marshall dropped down from an overhead platform, a pistol in one hand pointed at her. He was far more imposing and intimidating in person than on TV, his ice-cold blue eyes revealing an iron will of a warrior on mission, even as his mouth smiled with bemused approval.

"Why, Secretary Sachs, is that a standard-issue U.S. military sidearm you're waving at me?" he said. "I didn't know you had it in you. Better be careful, you might hurt yourself."

Sachs raised her gun at Marshall. "I will kill you, Marshall."

"I've already given my life for my country," he said, taking a step forward. "You think I'm not ready to die to see this through? I'm a patriot."

"Of course you are, Marshall. You're the Great American Pretender."

"Defender, Sachs," Marshall said sharply, his smile disappearing. "Defender."

"Defender," she repeated, trying to put everything together that she had seen. "You were so confident we could win this war with minimal casualties."

"Maybe we can," Marshall said.

The radio crackled. "Defender Ten, all clear."

"Defender Nine, all clear."

Sachs realized Marshall had established the secret frequency she needed to recall the Defenders. If only she could reach the radio. "You actually built your Defender system, didn't you?"

Marshall cracked a grin. "I've got ten airborne COIL lasers that can pinpoint and destroy enemy missiles hundreds of miles away."

"So you blew up Washington?" Sachs said accusingly.

Marshall grew scarily calm, but his eyes were ablaze with purpose. "It was clean, Sachs. I took out buildings. Not people."

"What do you call four thousand Americans?"

"Not much more than 9/11," he said. "And what do you call the hundreds of thousands who died worldwide from the Chinese pandemic? Hell, millions for all we know in China alone. Any reasonable president would have launched under attack. But you wouldn't."

"So you blew up SAC headquarters," she said. "And you went after my daughter!"

"Something worth thinking about now, Sachs, if you want her to live."

Marshall took another step closer, and Sachs took a step back. Suddenly she wondered why he hadn't killed her yet.

"What do you want with her, Marshall?"

"Just a little leverage," Marshall said, raising his gun to her head. "I might need you to make one more address about your attack on the Chinese."

"Oh, my God," she said, realizing that Marshall—and history—was going to blame this apocalypse on her failed leadership.

"You're going to take a bullet for America, Sachs," he told her. "You think the Chinese care about human rights? Ask the people of Hong Kong. You think they care about inclusion and diversity? They don't even believe in the transcendence of the human soul. The individual doesn't exist to them, only the collective. Even Carver would tell you they're the Borg."

"If he were still alive."

"I have to protect western civilization, Sachs. Before people like you piss it away. Now hand over the gun. We both know you can't pull the trigger."

She felt the veins in her hand throb as she gripped the gun. She could barely catch her breath, her heart was racing so fast. One way or another, she told herself, she was going to take a bullet. Whether she took the shot or not, she was going to die. She had to take the shot. She had to pull the trigger.

"Those who can't, teach," Marshall said, coaxing her. "Come on. Give it to me."

Sachs, her hands trembling, started to lower her arms. He was only a few feet away now, more confident than ever, his hand swinging up with his gun.

Sachs jerked up her gun and fired three times fast, one bullet snapping his head back, the others catching him in the chest, driving him against his radar equipment. He bounced off and fell onto the liner plate floor, a stream of blood trickling into a crack like waste in a gutter.

Hands trembling, gun smoking, she dropped the pistol on the floor with a clank.

"Decapitation, Marshall. Your own philosophy."

Marshall was lifeless. Powder burns surrounded the black hole in his forehead. His piercing blue eyes remained wide open in surprise. Sachs stood there numb, staring at Marshall, her heart sick, her stomach upside down.

The crackle of the radio broke her trance: "Defender One, update."

Sachs staggered over to the console. She felt weak as she grasped the microphone with her hand and then saw blood on it. She looked down at her body. More blood. Somewhere along the line she already had taken a bullet. Now she had to recall the Defenders before that bullet took her last breath.

CHAPTER FIFTY-SEVEN

1649 Hours
The Pacific
Northern Command

High over the Pacific Ocean, ten 747 jumbo jets were strung out like white pearls in the moonlight. Inside their respective cockpits, President Deborah Sachs' very weak voice came through the secret frequency: "Arm your phasers," she said. "Target is now U.S. Minutemen missiles entering Chinese airspace. Repeat. Target is now ten U.S. missiles entering Chinese airspace."

Inside Northern Command, General Block heard her too, thanks to the Defender One pilot who was patching everything through for verification since General Marshall had ceased transmission.

"Good God," Block told his senior controller. "They're really up there, fully operational. Ten actual airborne Defenders."

"They're requesting confirmation for the destruction of outgoing U.S. missiles in place of potential incoming Chinese missiles," the senior controller said.

Even now, Block realized, elements of his own armed forces still refused to heed the words of their new commander-in-chief. "You tell them they heard right."

Floating at 35,000 feet, Defender One swung into position. Mounted on its nosecone, a large swiveling laser cannon turret containing a beam director and infrared sensor scanned the horizon for missile launches.

The beam director shot a low-powered laser beam to track the missiles and measure atmospheric distortion.

Meanwhile, inside the forward fuselage of the Defender, a mirror adjusted while the displays of a computer console flashed. One display read Atmospheric Distortion 34.222. Another display read: missile tracking: locked.

The mirror locked into place.

Inside the rear fuselage of Defender One, walls of transparent storage tanks lined both sides of a narrow aisle—30,000 pounds of chemicals moving at supersonic speeds, mixed in a rocket engine-like chamber. A flash in the mix lit up and shot through the clear shaft.

The laser burst out through the beam director in the nosecone of the 747.

Over the Pacific Ocean, the first Minuteman exploded over black waters.

Not cheers but stunned silence lay like a cloud over the Northern Command headquarters as one by one the blips representing Minuteman missiles coming down on China disappeared.

Block exhaled with both admiration and horror. "Goddamn Marshall."

It didn't take long for General Zhang to call.

Block picked up his red phone. "What do you want, Zhang?"

Zhang said in perfect American English, "We wish to cease hostilities."

"I'm sure you do." It was all Block could do to keep from calling him "Charlie," but he refrained out of respect for President Sachs. "You saw that we can destroy our own missiles, General. Which means we can destroy yours too."

Zhang continued, "We suggest an immediate, verifiable cease-fire."

"Lucky for you, President Sachs agrees. But she wants a long-term, verifiable treaty we'll work out later. Maybe include those artificial atolls you've got in the South China Sea."

"Agreed." Zhang said. "Over."

Before Zhang cut off, Block heard what sounded like a few curse words in Mandarin. He then hung up and looked at his senior controller, who was fluent in Mandarin. "What did he say?"

"He said, 'Tough broad.' More or less, sir."

"You got that right," Block said, smiling. "Tell President Sachs we've got teams from Grand Forks on the way to provide her with medical attention."

But his senior controller said, "She's not responding anymore, sir."

CHAPTER FIFTY-EIGHT

1650 Hours
Bedford Country Club

Jennifer struggled as the Green Beret on top of her forced her down onto the floor of the caddy shack, one hand grabbing her hair and the other pawing at her breasts. She still had clothes on, nothing torn open yet, thank God. This drunken perv had only dry humped her so far, but his grinding repulsed her like nothing before in her life.

"This isn't the frickin' Islamic State!" she screamed, kneeing him in the groin. "You can't just rape girls!"

He bellowed in agony but didn't let go of her, pulling her tighter until she winced in pain. "Oh, I'm going to like you," he told her, forcing his mouth on hers.

Gagging, she reached for his empty bottle on the floor beside them. Her fingers fumbled, then grasped it by the neck but couldn't get a firm hold. She was about to lose it as he shifted on her.

She grimaced, then slipped her tongue into his mouth and he came alive. She used the moment to grab the bottle and club him across the side of his head.

"Bitch!" he cried out, staggering to the side as she hit him again, sending him face down on the floor.

"Believe it, asshole!" She kicked him out of the way, the rage in her so strong that this time instead of opening the front door, she just kicked it open with little difficulty and ran out to blazing lights and guns and froze.

A dark, knife-thin figure emerged from the lights, like one of those aliens from the movies.

"Jennifer, I'm Wanda Randolph of the United States Capitol Police. Your mother sent me to help you. She's alive."

Jennifer wanted to cry like a baby. Instead she fixed her eyes on the long sniper rifle in Randolph's hands. "That's a sweet Barrett M107 50-caliber. Can I hold it?"

CHAPTER FIFTY-NINE

0631 Hours
The Day After
The Safeguard Complex

It was the 91st Security Forces Squadron team who reached Sachs first at the Safeguard complex. She was unconscious on the floor under a console, her clothes, hands and hair a bloody mess. But she was breathing, and they stabilized her quickly then moved her outside.

As dawn broke over the 80-foot pyramid radar building, she blinked her eyes open into the cold light of day. It seemed like there were hundreds of soldiers, federal agents and FEMA officials on hand. News crews too, although they had been fenced off beyond the base.

"What's going on?" she asked.

"You," said a familiar voice. "You'll be just fine. But we'll need to airlift you for surgery to get that bullet out of you. I got lucky. Mine passed clean through."

She looked over to see Koz, his left shoulder bandaged up. "Koz." She paused. "And Captain Li?"

Koz shook his head, clearly broken up. "Last official casualty of the attack. But it's over, thanks to you."

There was a shout, and a soldier ran up with a phone for Koz. "General Block, sir."

Koz took the phone and said, "Captain Li is dead, sir. So is Marshall."

Sachs could hear Block's shocked voice on the other end. "You killed Marshall?"

"No, sir," Koz said, looking at her. "She did."

"Sachs?" Block repeated, even louder.

"Yes, sir."

"Well, I'll be damned."

There were more shouts and the snow kicked up. Sachs looked around, bewildered. Suddenly a Black Hawk chopper landed on the missile field. Her body instantly seized up in terror. Then the chopper's big door slid open and out jumped a tall, thin Black female officer. And right behind her was Jennifer, running toward her.

"Mom!" Jennifer called. "Mom!"

Jennifer ran up to her and embraced her. Sachs cried her eyes out, kissing Jennifer all over, squeezing her until her baby could barely breathe. "Oh, baby."

Koz had to gingerly pry them apart.

Jennifer straightened and looked over Koz once, then twice, and without disappointment. She must have seen something, because she smiled and saluted him.

Koz returned the salute with his right arm, and Jennifer gave her mom a big thumbs-up, as if to say that, despite everything that had happened, America was going to be OK.

CHAPTER SIXTY

0900 Hours
Three Weeks Later
Looking Glass

Koz sat in the conference room of the Looking Glass plane watching the ceremonies on TV. They were raising the U.S. Constitution from the bowels of the earth where the National Archives once stood, and he noted how regal President Sachs looked as a large crane lifted the indestructible container with the sacred document into the air. But to Koz, it was sacred only so long as it lived in the hearts of Americans, like Deborah Sachs lived in his.

He was so mesmerized by the scene that he didn't notice his new communications officer walk in.

"General Kozlowski?"

Koz glanced over at Captain Lyndon Han, who was holding his digital tablet and pen out for a signature. Han was a fine officer, but no Captain Li. But then nobody could truly replace her in his eyes. Koz signed off the checklist on the tablet and handed it back.

Han nodded at the TV. "Dinner at the president's again tonight, sir?"

"No," Koz said, brightening. "I'm cooking."

As he spoke, his phone buzzed with a text message. Only a few people besides the president were ever allowed to get through to him up here.

"Excuse me, Captain," he said, looking at the text.

It was from Jennifer Sachs: *R u really grilling 2nite? Count me in! :)*

He stared at the text for a long minute. He could barely comprehend the tragic, terrible twist of fate that had created his new nuclear family from the ashes of a nuclear attack. He lost himself for a moment, remembering Sherry and so many others who perished in Washington. He should have been one of them, if not for Captain Li. Hell, they all would have perished were it not for Deborah Sachs.

Then his comm beeped with an FYI about a glitch in the VLF extension that he really needn't worry about and his trance was broken.

"I better have a look at that myself," he replied, taking no glitch for granted since encountering Red Glare.

As he rose from his chair and stood up, he looked out the compartment window and smiled. The Looking Glass plane was moving up and away above the clouds, its starboard wing reflecting the glint of a new day's sun against clear blue skies.

BOOKS BY THOMAS GREANIAS

Gods of Rome

The 34th Degree

The Promised War

The Atlantis Revelation

The Atlantis Prophecy

Raising Atlantis

ABOUT THOMAS GREANIAS

Thomas Greanias is the acclaimed *New York Times* bestselling author of ten international adventures, including the *Raising Atlantis* trilogy, *Gods of Rome,* and *Red Glare.* CBS News calls his work "gripping page-turners you stay up way too late reading." The *Washington Post* says, "Greanias writes captivating roller coasters that penetrate the biggest mysteries of our times." Thomas is a graduate of Northwestern University, where he studied national security, journalism and fiction writing. He lives by the beach with his family and golden retriever.

Printed in Poland
by Amazon Fulfillment
Poland Sp. z o.o., Wrocław

23393425R00165